Blood Moon

Wildcat Wizard Book 1

Get deals and new releases notifications first via the
newsletter www.alkline.co.uk

Bit of a Bind

My stomach fluttered with a thousand butterflies as the rope that bound my feet slipped over the accelerator pedal and the car sped up. I struggled but it just made it worse.

"Pepper," I said calmly to my companion, "would you mind yanking very hard on the handbrake before we crash into the wall in front of us?"

"Use the brake," he squealed, eyes wide, arms braced on the dashboard.

"My feet are caught."

"Can't you get them free?" I turned to him and raised an eyebrow. "Sorry, just thought I'd ask."

"Just pull the bloody handbrake," I screamed, the side wall of a block of garages getting perilously close.

"You do it," said Pepper. "You'll only moan if I do it wrong."

"Wrong? It's a wall, and we'll hit it. How wrong can you do it?"

"You sure?"

Sometimes, just now and then, Pepper really got on my chakras. "Yes!" I nudged my head, indicating my hands that were rather annoyingly tied to the steering wheel.

"Ah, yeah. Sorry, forgot," said Pepper with a sheepish grin.

"DO IT!"

"Just don't get mad. You know what you're like when you get angry. You go all blasty with your wand."

"I'll blast you if you don't fu—"

He did it.

I tried to keep control, but the whole hands being tied thing was an issue. And, to be honest, I hadn't thought things through properly.

"Oops," I said. What can I say? I'm a master of understatement.

Tires screeched then we bucked sideways. The car jumped in the air like a frog shot out of a miniature cannon, and we somersaulted what felt like fifty times but was probably once before landing. "Argle," I said, before we rolled down the road for a hundred yards, hitting the wall anyway. It's things like this that give me a headache, especially after the morning I'd already had.

You'd think having the local goons tie you to the steering wheel while they ransack your vehicle for a certain item you may have accidentally borrowed without asking would be enough for a morning, but it was just the start.

When Pepper snuck into the car while they were otherwise occupied and pressed the starter, I drove away very fast as it seemed like the smart move to make. But no, turns out it was the opposite of smart.

Dumb. That's the word. Very, very dumb.

Being upside down in a car after hitting a wall gives you a whole new perspective on not just the street but life in general.

I was considering maybe my best course of action for the future was not to get caught again. That's the one drawback to being a criminal even in a world of criminals—sometimes the bad guys are after you more than the cops. At least in prison you get fed and given a nice cozy room to call your own. In my world all you get is hit repeatedly about the head with heavy objects, then dumped in the nearest canal, usually with your hands tied to yet another heavy object.

Blood poured into eyes, meaning either my head was bleeding or I was still upside down and it was my nose dripping copious amounts of tangy life ketchup. Yup, my nose. What a downer. It had been fixed less than a year ago, now it would be all wonky again. It's an issue for us large-nosed guys, but it makes me distinguished, I guess, so what you gonna do?

Pepper moaned and groaned and generally overreacted beside me, then pulled out his little knife and cut the cords that bound me.

"Why the hell didn't you do that earlier? You utter pleb," I said.

"Sorry, didn't think."

"Quiet, it was rhetorical. Er, actually, no, it wasn't. Damn, let's get out of here."

We clambered out the car, thankfully not mine, another "borrow," and I found there was an upside to crashing into a wall. The goons were gone, scared off by the bit of bother, so that was nice.

"Grab the duffel," I told Pepper, who scowled then hobbled to the back of the car.

"Did you disable the wards?" he asked with a squeal.

"Damn, no, sorry. Give me a mo." I let my mind clear and reality dissolved as my focus crept to the magic wards I'd placed around the bag to stop anyone else taking it. In my mind's eye, they floated away from where they were stuck to the soft leather handle and winked out of existence. I left the rest in place, just freeing up enough for Pepper to carry it. It helped to picture them like that, although it's just a way to maintain focus. "Okay," I said, "we're good to go. Just hold the handle carefully and don't touch the rest of the bag."

After a little more grumbling about not signing up to get dissolved by magic because I was forgetful, and that I should trust him, Pepper managed to get the goods and held the large, tan leather duffel carefully in his hand. It was a nice bag, but its contents were what interested me. It had been one hell of a job to get it and I was kinda wishing I hadn't bothered. All it had caused me was trouble. It seemed every gangster in the country wanted what was inside, whatever that may have been.

Time to go.

I scratched at my head, surprised it was still there, then I went cold, true dread tickling my spine like the time I met this woman with six... Never mind. "My hat! Damn. Wait here." I rushed back to the car, scrambled inside, and found the pork pie hat. It had been through as much as me, was my oldest and dearest friend, and there it was. A perfectly brushed tan hat, dark brown band with a single feather on the left poking above the ribbon, a small silver trinket pinned there the day I got it.

Back out the car, I put Grace—all hats should have a name, it's respectful—where she belonged and ran back to Pepper, only now feeling whole again.

"What now?" he asked.

I studied my skinny friend for a moment, wondering how a criminal mastermind such as myself, a man who'd made it his duty for many years to steal other people's stuff that they didn't deserve to have, had been lumbered with a sidekick so peculiar as he. I shuddered at the thought, but knew it was because I genuinely liked the guy. Even if he had the morals of a fish and stank worse.

"Now? Now, we run. Can you smell that?"

Pepper sniffed, blunt nose twitching, then shook his head. "Just the stink of the garbage."

"No, the duffel. Did you do something? Why's it glowing?" I stared at the bag, a fierce spectral light emanating from inside.

Pepper freaked. Some would say overreacted.

"No!" I shouted, but it was too late.

He flung the bag as hard as possible and I watched in dismay, already pining over the sure-to-be-forfeit bounty, as it sailed through the air and landed on the car's fuel tank.

"Um, I done bad, right?" said Pepper.

"Yes, Pepper," I sighed, "you done very bad."

The bag shone brighter, clearly unamused by being manhandled, and sparkled and crackled wildly as the intense light from within became almost blinding.

"How're your legs?" I asked. Pepper stared down at the scrawny appendages. I just sighed and ran away.

"Hey, wait!" He ran after me, and then our world was consumed with noise and heat as we were thrown fifty yards down the potholed street.

"Glad I got my hat," I said before I lost consciousness for the second time that day.

It was only nine AM; the day was not off to a good start.

Hi, I'm Arthur "The Hat" Salzman, but you can call me Arthur. Unless, of course, you have a job for me. Then just don't call at all, okay?

I'm kinda busy.

Why Gangsters Hate Wizards

You know when you graze your hands and they get all gritty under the skin and for a moment you stare at them as if they aren't your own? They're numb and you think, "Ah, cool, bits to tease out later, and it doesn't even sting?" This wasn't one of those times. My hands hurt like I had half a road under the heels and my face hadn't fared much better, although at least I couldn't see it. Bonus.

The shockwave was bad, but we were alive, and that was always a good sign. It meant I could keep on running. We got to our feet and I checked Pepper and he me—there were no smoldering clothes, so at least we weren't about to combust. Another bonus.

What wasn't a bonus was the fact Pepper had thrown my prize away and it had caused a fireball. I had a good mind to slap him but my palm hurt too much.

First things first, so I called on the strength within and watched with satisfaction as the gravel and dirt popped out my hands and tinkled to the rain-soaked road. A moment later, the skin sealed over and the pain receded. Focusing on my face, I winced as more lumps of jagged asphalt dropped back where they belonged.

Then I slapped Pepper across the back of the head.

"Ow!" Pepper rubbed at his lumpy bonce but had the presence of mind to look abashed, and well he might.

"Do you know what I was gonna get for that?"

"No. What?"

"Shut up, it was rhetorical."

"Are you sure?" he asked, eyes scrunched up, studying me like I was about to grow another head.

"Yes." I wasn't, but I didn't tell him that.

The car was burning fiercely, but when I sent out feelers for the wards around the bag my spirits soared as they answered loud and clear.

Yes! My protection had stopped the flames from devouring the leather and, more importantly, the contents.

Nigel was adamant he had to have this, and no way was I one to disappoint him, especially when it came to promises of rich rewards and maybe even a bonus.

We approached the car with caution, then waited with mounting impatience and a good deal of nervousness—as the goons would be sure to return—for the fire to die down.

It's surprising how quickly a car can burn out, which was good as we weren't still inside and I wasn't known for my patience. Unable to wait any longer, I took a chance and jumped up on the scalding chassis, grabbed the bag, and hopped back down.

"Come on. Let's get out of here before the goons come back."

"Can't believe you let them catch you like that. Pretty amateurish, Arthur."

"I was waiting for you, you cheeky git. And you were late, as usual."

"Sorry, I was doing my hair."

I inspected the study in chaos on top of his head and wondered exactly what he'd done to it, then dismissed it as one of those unsolvable cases. I had other things to worry about besides my buddy's fashion sense, or lack of.

"So, how did they get you and tie you up? You're a wizard, why didn't you blast their asses?"

"I fell asleep. Didn't get more than an hour last night what with all the getting of the item. And, er, well, they drugged me. Must have used the new stuff I've been hearing about. I can't very well blast 'em if I'm unconscious."

It was becoming increasingly difficult to be an honest criminal. Other like-minded, enterprising souls, those with half a brain, were getting inventive. Rather than punch you unconscious—which is fine for those without magic but very risky to try on those like me— they were getting smart and just injecting their victims before doing what they wished. In my case, that was tying me up while they searched for the item. Then I had no doubt they would have done something much more lethal once they knew they had what they wanted and had then worked out how to deal with it.

"Could've stayed awake," said Pepper, then sauntered off. Sauntering was a good idea, so I jogged to catch up. Time to finish this business and get paid.

We wandered down the center of the road, unconcerned about police as we weren't in the most enviable of areas. Same for any regular folks. They'd keep quiet unless expressly invited to talk by one of the many gangsters soon to arrive.

Those watching would have seen a sight many had seen before. Namely, Pepper and I.

Pepper was a scrawny dude with dirty blond hair always thick with one new product or other, eyes rather pink-rimmed and pale blue like faded denim that was, possibly, cool in the eighties, his skin color as stonewashed as his eyes. He had a strange, springy gait, like everything he walked on was bouncy.

Me, I usually sported three-day stubble and had pale blue eyes with a dark ring around the iris that made people double-take as it looked odd. The ring of magic all adepts have, grows thicker and darker the longer you practice and the more magic you can control. I favored lightweight linen shirts, as this business often got sweaty, usually tucked into a brown leather belt with an expensive, yet unpretentious buckle.

I wore cargo pants almost exclusively as they're not only comfortable and look good but you can never have too many pockets, and I'd worn the same soft leather boots for almost as long as my hat.

A few bracelets and dark brown, shoulder length hair with a slight curl completed what I liked to think of as an understated but still stylish look.

Not forgetting my hat. I love my hat.

My musings concerning the figures we cut to those watching from behind twitching curtains were cut short.

"Wonder what it is?" whispered Pepper, glancing at the bag as if it might be eavesdropping. Hell, for all I knew it was.

"Don't peek, you'll regret it. Remember that time with the imp and you just had to open the lid, didn't you? Took months for me to get my hearing back. I couldn't use the telephone for ages. Do you know how hard it is to order pizza when you can't hear? I kept getting bloody pineapple on them. Pineapple!"

"I said I was sorry."

"You, my little friend, are too nosy by half."

"Can't help it. It's what I do, I'm known for it. It's my thing."

"My thing is staying alive, so don't peek. Come on, let's get outta here."

It was right around this time that the goons returned. One minute no goons, next minute goonageddon. Story of my life.

A slender length of polished wood was in my hands as if by magic—haha—when in reality I just slid it from the specially made deep pocket on the right thigh of my cargo pants. As the power it helped focus welled up inside of me, I saw the truth behind all things. Saw the thoughts, few as they were, swirling in the air above the heads of the goons like wibbly-wobbly signposts, saying, "Let's break lots of Arthur's bits off and stomp on them. Let's stomp on them good."

So I killed them.

Don't think bad of me. They were nasty goons, not nice goons, and besides, nobody got to stomp on me, not unless I paid for it, and I gave that up years ago when people began to talk.

We ran away then, as that's what you do when gangsters have found you and want what you have. Especially when those gangsters happen to be big and work for someone even bigger.

Halfway down the street there was an almighty kerfuffle from behind and we turned to see more large men in ill-fitting clothes get out of a car and head our way.

"Guess everyone's up early," I muttered.

"Maybe you should be more discreet," said Pepper.

"Shut up," I said. "You're the one who blew up the car."

I waved what really was just a nice stick, but helped me to focus power and to be honest just made me feel more wizardly, and made suitably threatening noises. Pepper insulted them in his mother tongue, and they did the sensible thing. Stayed put.

The sigils on the waxy wood glowed with a pale light. Sigils I'd designed myself, personal to me and a shortcut to summoning spells that had got me out of more sticky situations than I cared to remember. The air crackled and with a final flourish as the magic retreated

I slid my wand back into its narrow pocket, adjusted my hat, and gave the goons one last hard stare. They may have got the better of me earlier, but they knew better than to mess with me when awake, unless I was drained of magic.

With a practiced sneer, we turned to be on our merry way, and walked straight into two fists. One each.

It's all well and good being able to wield elemental forces and face down otherworldly creatures, but when I'm unconscious I'm still about as dangerous as a sack of rotten potatoes. I just smell nicer.

I'm the kind of criminal criminals hate as I have a conscience. As long as it doesn't interfere with me getting paid, of course.

And then I was being dragged into a car and taken to see Boris, local Boss and not my best friend. Our meetings usually went something like this: "Um, can you stop hitting me now?" I say.

"No," he says.

See, less than ideal.

Didn't See That Coming

I've been tied up, shot, stabbed, killed a few times, had bits chopped off—luckily nothing important—been flayed a little, spat at a lot, punched more times than I've had hot dinners, and kicked even more.

I've been called names, too, but sticks and stones and all that.

So being strung up by my arms and repeatedly hit in various exposed places was nothing new, but it still hurt like a mo-fo, same as always.

"Hey. Ugh. HEY!"

Mike the goon paused his pounding and I spiraled in a lazy arc a foot above the ground, going from dark to blinding light as I spun to face the ridiculously powerful light shining in my face. Boris did love the drama, I think he took gangster acting classes or something.

Same could be said for his goon. He had his gooniness down to an art, proper pro in every regard.

"What?" he grunted in a suitably deep and menacing way.

"Can you stop punching me in the kidneys? It really smarts."

"Shut it, Arthur. I've got me orders, and me orders are to tenderize you good."

"I'm already tender, honest. Look, feel. As soft as your mummy's titties—Ugh."

Mike kept on hitting me. I kept on grunting.

"Why has he got his hat on?" roared Boris as he came down the steps of the cellar, emerging from the dark in an appropriately dramatic and, I guess, intimidating manner—his trademark muscles were very much in evidence.

He wore a t-shirt of his latest sponsor, some fitness outfit I'd never heard of. Boris was constantly swapping brands, wearing an ever-changing supply of jogging pants, vests, hoodies, trainers, and even sports bracelets. Striking poses and showing them off at every opportunity. It was weird, but apparently was how companies sold their gear. Social media was the new TV advert.

These companies were smart and getting smarter, sponsoring anyone who had a following, and boy did Boris. He was about as well known as they came in our world, but that was nothing compared to his online presence. Apparently, gangster bodybuilders were cool, and Boris made some serious cash by showing off his muscles and his latest gear to his several-million-strong virtual tribe.

It wasn't just because of the jacked, steroid-boosted muscles, the implants, or the ridiculous proportions of his body. No, it was because he was a mean bastard and played up to the camera.

But none of that was his main business, just a sideline so he could get the attention he craved. His real business was drugs, so what he was doing chasing after magical artifacts was anyone's guess.

Mike, the goon, said, "I couldn't get it off," and at least had the sense to look embarrassed.

"Arthur, are you messing with Mike again?" scalded Boris, waggling a finger at me. Even his fingers were well-muscled.

"Sorry, couldn't resist," I wheezed, the slight smile on my lips making my ribs hurt. I was sure something cracked.

Boris tutted and stepped forward, stopping in just the right spot so his muscles were shown off to best effect. "What you got in the bag, eh?" he asked, licking his lips.

"No idea."

"Come on, you're amongst friends here, buddy. Let old Boris in on the gig. I'll make it worth your while."

"No can do, I'm afraid," I said, knowing things could get a lot worse if my broker didn't get what I'd agreed to deliver.

"Hmm." Boris thinking was never a good sign. He wasn't big on pontificating, and his pondering usually resulted in him telling Mike to keep on pounding until the meat became fully tenderized.

"Tell you what," I said, "how about you let me go and I don't break every bone in Mike here's body and maybe rip your freaky arms off while I'm at it?"

"Are you out of your tiny fucking mind, Arthur?" Boris flexed a bicep as if to prove no way could I remove it.

"No, I'm not, but I've had it with you guys. This is the final straw. I've let you have your fun over the years, Boris, but when you try to steal my stuff and beat the living crap out of my friends, well, enough's enough. I'm warning you, you too, Mike. Let us go or our truce is well and truly over."

Boris flexed again, but I saw the doubt, the confusion. I'd never spoken to him like that before, and it was rash and stupid, but he'd crossed a line you didn't cross unless you were willing to see it through to the end, and boy did he have a long way to go if he wanted to deal with me.

He knew this, was merely pushing his luck because he was neither the boss nor the man he once was. Others were gaining ground, the battles for territory getting increasingly violent, and we'd always spoken to each other with politeness until now—he knew what I was capable of, and me him. Brutal and stupid, a very bad combination.

"No deal." Boris swallowed as he ambled back into the shadows and said, "Mike, break the runt's legs. Then shatter his kneecaps then cut his fingers off. If Arthur doesn't cooperate after that, then kill Pepper and begin on the wizard." Boris was a believer. He didn't understand how it worked, but he believed. Had seen things that gave him no choice.

"I warned you," I shouted. "I warned you a long time ago to stay out of my way. You know the deal, Boris, you know I won't stand for..." A door slammed so I stopped talking.

Mike grinned at me and said, "It's about time the boss decided to deal with you. You're a pain in the ass, Arthur, and so is your little buddy here." Mike wandered over to Pepper, strung up like me, silent and unafraid even faced with the goon and his orders.

"Pepper, I think now would be a good time to smash this guys face in, waddya think?"

"I think that's a very good idea, Arthur, very good."

People like Mike and his boss didn't really understand me, or others in my world, and were too caught up in their own warped version of reality to ever accept it. They were low level, relied on fear and fists, and believed magic was mostly for little tricks and cool stuff, not anything that would threaten their way of life, certainly not their actual lives. I'd never been one to tell them different.

Mike here was about to find out the truth about what happened when you really pissed off a wizard.

"Say goodbye to your legs," sneered Mike as he picked up a sledgehammer leaning against the wall.

"Say goodbye to your face," I whispered.

Mike tested his grip with the sledgehammer, hefted it over his shoulder, and grunted as he swung it fast and hard at Pepper's kneecap. See, he couldn't even follow orders. It was break legs first, then kneecaps, not the other way round.

Silence enveloped me for a split second that felt like a lifetime, out of time and place, the nothingness. The elements were there for me to control, within reason, and I focused my thoughts, became at one with the room and the air it contained.

It was kinda weird not using my wand, almost like a limb was missing, but I did a good enough job.

As the sledgehammer arced toward Pepper's knee, the wind came from nowhere and I turned my head, directing the air as I willed it to bend to my will. The sledgehammer changed direction under terrible pressures and missed Pepper's leg, kept on moving in an altered arc at a speed impossible to stop. Before Mike was able to let go of the handle it smacked him square in the face, pulverizing his nose, shattering his teeth, caving in the entire front of his head and splitting his skull wide open.

He was very much dead as he crashed to the floor with a dull thud, the hammer wedged tight into his obliterated face.

Focus still centered on Pepper, ignoring Mike for now, I let the air relax and instead turned the elements into a very different combination. The air danced and sparkled as the rope holding up Pepper smoldered. Then it burned with a fierce flame that died almost immediately. I was already low on power and this was the final act, and hardly sufficient.

Pepper dangled there for a moment with the rope frayed, then it split with a twang and he dropped, remarkably gracefully, to the floor.

He scrambled over to the table and found his knife in the pile of our clothes and quickly cut the bonds around his hands.

"Idiot," he said, as he kicked Mike in the ribs. Pepper had a mean streak, but was a good guy.

"Guess Boris is no longer our friend, Pepper," I said as he came over to cut me down.

"Guess not. Shame, I kinda liked him."

"He goes too far. There are limits."

"Sorry about this," said Pepper, standing in front of me and staring at the knife like it was something he'd never seen before.

"Hey, buddy, it's not your fault."

"No, I mean about this." And with that Pepper stabbed me in the heart.

Dying sucks, especially when it's a friend that kills you.

Why Wasn't I Scared?

Almost every day I died a mini-death. I welcomed it with open arms. It was my release, my chance to unwind. To forget my troubles, relax and let the cares of the world pass me by, no concern of mine.

I embraced the oblivion, the freedom from myself, and if I never woke up in the morning I wouldn't mind. How could I?

Sleep is such a beautiful thing, yet also a poignant reminder of the transient nature of a personal existence everyone seems to feel will continue forever. As if they can somehow avoid the inevitable and be the first person to live until the end of all things.

Not me, I knew what sleep really was. Practice for the real thing. Every single night of your life you are no longer you. You switch off, all conscious thought gone, and you die only to be reborn the very next morning. Waking full of worry and woe, stressing about this or that before you're even out of bed. Fretting over if you let the cat out or if there's milk or if maybe today is the day you finally fall sleep and never wake up.

I told myself all of this every night when I put Grace on my bedside table and wound my watch. I reminded myself that death was nothing to fear, merely a long sleep, and who's afraid of sleeping? That's all death is, just a big old vacation from the trials and tribulations of the woken mind.

Quiet.

Oh, how blissful to have stillness of the mind. To sleep and be empty of hurt and pain. I craved it, needed it. But it seldom came. I could not sleep, I could not rest, I could not always die the mini-death when I needed it the most. Arthur the insomniac. The blissful release eluded me so often, leaving me to live my life in a waking dream not of my own design. Boundaries became blurred if it got too bad, and I was prone to falling asleep at the most inopportune moments when the weariness overwhelmed me.

Oh, for the death of a full night's sleep. Such a wondrous gift so many take for granted.

Being killed, like made properly dead, is different, though. Much more final. No waking to thoughts of toast and marmalade, a cup of tea and then out to start your day.

As Pepper slid the knife into my heart, the blade wasn't what hurt, it was the betrayal.

Death's one thing, death by sidekick quite another.

Know what my last thought was?

I wondered what the hell was in the bag.

Yeah, sucky, right? A wild life full of magic and intrigue and no end of gangster stuff and my last thought was about a damn bag. It must have been something amazing and incredibly valuable to warrant Pepper's betrayal.

At this point I'd died five times in my life, and every time I did it came as a real surprise, proper shocker. I was prepared mentally, accepted that it could be my last moment on earth for real, no coming back this time, but it never ceased to be a real downer. It does something to your head, something peculiar and inexplicable.

You see things.

Strange things.

The other side.

And the other side was not a place I wanted to be right now.

"Again? This is getting old, Arthur," chastised Death.

"Tell me about it," I said with a sigh, knowing none of it was real, that it was just my dying mind playing tricks before it shut down because my heart was punctured and I was basically dead.

"Okay, what was it this time? Another wizard? An accident? I told you to be more careful around cars, they're dangerous."

"No, Imaginary Figure of Death, none of those. I got well and truly murdered by a buddy. Nasty stuff, and a bit of a blow, haha, if I'm honest."

"Oh, that old chestnut. It's more common than you think. Did you know that most murders are committed by acquaintances?" Death smiled at me, nodding his head as if I was well keen to hear all his facts and figures.

"Um, can we talk about this another time? I'm, er, dead, bleeding out while I hang from a hook in a suitably atmospheric cellar. It's got water on the floor, deep shadows, bright spotlight, dead goon, the works. All that good stuff. I'd rather not die there and stay dead."

"Fine," said Death with a sigh, "but this is the last time."

"Haha, you always say that," I said with a smile that turned into one hell of a grimace as I jerked wildly, the magic inside my body rushing to rebuild punctured muscle even as the blade slipped back out of my some would say gristly flesh.

"That's not nice, Pepper," I said.

Pepper's eyes widened as he jumped back, a vein pumping erratically right in the middle of his forehead. "But... but, I just—"

"Yeah, yeah, killed me and thought you'd get away with the booty, I know. Damn traitor."

"Sorry, Arthur, but someone made me an offer I couldn't refuse."

"What, threatened your family or your friends did they?" I knew damn well he had no family and I was his only friend. Make that ex-friend.

"Um, no, mate. Offered me a shit load of cash. I'd be set for life."

"So, what, you were gonna steal the bag and whatever's inside and do a runner?"

"Summit like that, yeah," said Pepper, scratching his head, disturbing his stupid haircut, and still undecided about how to proceed. Bless him, if he wasn't so dense he could have got away with it, but he was forgetting one thing.

I was a bloody wizard!

Faery Godmother

Knowing I was in a less than ideal position to discuss the matter further, I did the sensible thing and kicked out hard. I hit him straight in the knackers. Goal! He moaned loudly and slumped to the floor like the toad he was, splashing into a puddle on the dirty, beer-stained concrete.

Pepper gasped and moaned but was already scrambling for his dropped knife.

Stilling my whirling mind, I focused the last of my magic on the knife and it sprang into the air moments before Pepper could reach it. As his head lifted in shock, my boot connected with his jaw. But it sent me spinning in a circle, getting a glimpse of Pepper out cold before I spun dizzily like a cannibal's lunch.

Fighting to control the knife, the elements loathe to cooperate with my waning strength, I carefully rested the blade against the unseen rope above me and felt rather than saw the edges fray.

With a *twang* I dropped the short distance to the floor.

The knife clattered and I reached for it. Time to release my hands and scarper before anything else went wrong. I was seriously regretting taking the job, and now it looked like I was down one sidekick and up one ruined body.

My ears rang as gunfire echoed around the cellar. I slammed flat to the wet floor as the wall behind me sprayed chips of concrete in all directions.

Again, a shot rang out, and Pepper's body juddered as a bullet smacked into the side of his head. Blood oozed out of a large exit wound, revealing his brain. Cold, gray, now empty of all he ever was and all he ever could have been. Guess it was the end of what had been some interesting times.

"You idiot," I whispered to Pepper. "We could have had a long career together."

Another shot almost blinded me as the floor right in front of me erupted with water and fractured concrete. I snatched the knife up with both hands and clutched it tight.

It's difficult to manhandle a knife when your hands are tied and you're feeling slightly panicked, but I got the blade facing the ropes and tried to saw my way to freedom. No easy task, but as soon as a few threads were severed the rest unraveled with ease, the blade cutting through as smoothly as it had my flesh.

Pepper's dead eyes stared at me as if in accusation, but what my crime was I had no idea. I certainly hadn't been the one to shoot him dead.

Hands free, but my body pinned down, I shouted, "Boris, can't we come to some kind of arrangement?"

"You killed Mike. He was my best goon and you killed him. Do you know how hard it is to get good goons?"

"Um, very?" I ventured. "And anyway, he was viciously beating on me, and you did tell him to kneecap Pepper."

"Details, details. Sorry, Arthur, you gotta die for this." Boris shot again so I shimmied close to Pepper to use him as a screen.

"No can do. I have an item to deliver and payment to collect."

"What is it?" he asked, unable to control his curiosity even now.

"No idea. All I know is that you aren't the only one after it and it sure as hell has everyone freaking. You mean to tell me after all this and you honestly have no idea what it is? Why did you want it, then?"

"Because someone gave me a load of cash and promised a lot more if I handed it over. Without looking."

"Oh, right. Fancy changing your mind?"

Boris fired again and this time it almost got me.

"Guess that's a no?" I shouted. Risking it, I rocked back onto my knees and threw the knife at the glaring spotlight.

The big guy may have been safe in the shadows, but as the bulb exploded the playing field was leveled. He fired wildly but now I could see where he was as the gun flashed.

I ran left away from Pepper and pinned myself against the wall, waiting.

I knew Boris, and he might be huge and tough, but he was also impatient. Plus, one more thing. He didn't like the dark.

Naked, just my hat on, I held my breath.

Sure enough, a few moments later he risked it and the table with my clothes and the duffel burst with light. Boris was highlighted with his hand on the bag's zipper, already recoiling with shock and pain as the magic wards protected what was mine, at least for a while.

He screamed in horror as his arm melted up to the elbow, flesh stripped away and bone shining in myriad colors as the magic did what I'd set it to do. Protect my stuff. He shot randomly, discharging the gun.

Once spent, I used the dying light to get to the table where Boris was now kneeling on the floor, arm little but bone and goop up to the shoulder, body slick with sweat and already deep in the throes of shock.

"You better get a doctor to see to that," I said, voice cold, no pity for the man that would have seen me dead.

"Go fu—"

Something slammed into the side of Boris' head and with a dull thud like a tree falling in a damp, mossy forest he toppled sideways, head split open and no longer worrying about his arm. Or anything else for that matter.

"You took your bloody time," I said to Sasha.

"And you're shriveled," she said staring down at my naked torso.

"Hey, it's the cold, all right? Come on, let's go."

"Where's Pepper?"

"Pepper's dead. Pepper is very, very dead."

I dressed quickly, Sasha silent beside me. She normally never stopped talking, but she was none too keen on what she called my "dirty business." With wand in pocket, hat on head, and mysterious bag slung over shoulder, I followed the glittering, swinging hips of Sasha up out of the cellar of Boris' bar, through the back door, and into daylight.

Death, A Real Inconvenience

There are many ways to die, and I've experienced a few. Trust me, one is more than enough.

Death number one was at the hands of Sasha, the beautiful—in an odd way—woman by my side. No, I don't hold it against her. She did me a favor. Some fae are skilled with potions and the old nice dress trick and pumpkins and whatnot—yes, you can go to the ball—others, like Sasha, have slightly darker, and less jolly arts. Are less inclined to turn rags into a nice sparkly gown, more inclined to send a swarm of chattering beasties after you from the Nolands.

She was about as dark as they came while still remaining on the right side of the Code, and it's a fine line she trod. Trust me, I know. I wibbled and wobbled across the tightrope between what's okay and what isn't myself.

Sasha came into my life at a critical moment. Namely, I was in a bit of a bind with let's just say an angry ex-owner of a certain object I'd reclaimed from him. He was less than impressed with my skills at sneaking and general thievery.

Sasha was bound to him and, gal of action that she was, took the opportunity to sever those ties in a very final way. She killed him, freeing herself, and then took it upon herself to do me a favor in return for my help. She gave me my first glimpse of the afterlife. She killed me, sending me into the first state of death.

It's not as bad as you might imagine, and there are certainly worse things, like state number two, which I have also experienced, but the first time is always the worst, and I have to admit it came as somewhat of a shock.

As I stared at the body of the dead guy, Sasha with a wicked grin on her face, she said she owed me a favor for allowing her a chance to gain her freedom.

I joked—only because I was nervous—saying to think nothing of it as long as she promised not to stop me taking back what I'd been paid to reclaim, but not ending up like the guy on the floor would be nice. She just smirked, her face lighting up like an angel's. How about immortality, or at least a taster of it? she'd asked me. Would I like to live forever? Die and come back, all that kind of thing?

I told her in no uncertain words that there was no way was I gonna be turned into a freaky vampire, but she tilted her head and laughed. A wild, free, dangerous laugh that made me smile but also sent shivers down my spine.

Silly little man, she'd said. No, nothing like that. No blood cravings, just the real deal. Regeneration without the side-effects. Magical, pure, untainted by any dark corruption. A taste of what it was to be fae.

And, like an idiot—I was younger then, rather wild if I'm honest—I said, sure, that sounded like fun.

So she killed me.

I thought she'd been joking. She was deadly serious.

One minute I was alive and rather surprised by the turn of events, the next I was very dead and having this oddball conversation with an imaginary Death just to stop myself going mad. I was back and gasping for air almost immediately, but it still felt like an eternity.

"What did you do?" I asked. She just shrugged her beautiful shoulders and smiled, making a zipper motion across her mouth.

It was only many weeks later that I found out she was my faery godmother. I know, right? Who'da thunk it?

The main drawback to having a faery godmother is that they're flaky as hell, or maybe it was just mine. I don't know, I have nothing to compare it to. Sasha came and went as she pleased, and mostly she pleased to stay away and let me get stabbed or hit or shot or slashed, sometimes all three in succession. Once, all at the same time. Occasionally, if I was lucky, the order changed just to mix it up and keep me on my toes.

All my deaths since the first had been different, not quite the final passing like the original should have been, but more akin to an advance screening of what the real thing would be like. I went, passed over, but the instant I died my body was already hard at work repairing the damage. As long as it wasn't my brain, then I could return, body healed so fast it was almost like it never happened.

But there were limits to this stuff, and one day I knew I'd find out what they were. I asked Sasha once how many goes I had at this thing called life. How many rebirths was I granted. She focused on me in a peculiar way and said, "I can't tell you that, Arthur. If you knew how many chances you had you'd get complacent. Take it for granted. Each death might be the final one. You may have one chance, you may have ten. All I can tell you is that one day you will die and never return. Keep that in mind."

So I tried not to be complacent and get myself killed. Sometimes it worked out, sometimes not. Think of it as Russian roulette, you can't go far wrong with that analogy. Rest assured, it's scary every damn time. I wouldn't recommend dying even once; it messes with your head something terrible.

Not wanting to hang around, I followed Sasha to her car and hopped in.

I also closed my eyes.

Sasha was, without doubt, the worst driver in the history of motoring. She refused to acknowledge other vehicles, believed stop lights were meant for mortals only, and speed limits were guidelines for people not in any kind of hurry, not actual rules to adhere to.

At least you got where you wanted to go quickly.

"Are you going to explain why you let some lowlifes capture you and steal your bag? I thought you were a good criminal? One that always delivered?"

"I am," I protested. "I'll have you know I have an impeccable record. Um, apart from that one time back east, and, er, there were a few issues several years ago but I was having problems with my hat and my magic was wonky. Oh, and there was the time that—Watch out!"

"You should be a better bad guy, Arthur. Not get caught or killed quite so often."

I don't think Sasha really understood the concept of being a criminal. She thought of it more as me getting into little scrapes and generally having fun. Although, to be fair, she was rather vague about the whole death thing, not really understanding what it was, or what she did to me when she gave me my gift.

"I try my best," I mumbled, feeling rather put out. I did pretty well, better than most. I was still alive for one, and that was more than most in our world could say.

Sasha kept her eyes on me as we sailed through the junction and were almost sideswiped, but, as usual, the other vehicles just bounced off us like we had an invisible forcefield around us, which was exactly what we did have.

Perks of being a faery, I guess.

Heading Home

I needed to change, and I needed to rest and get my magical strength back before I even attempted to deliver what I'd been paid to deliver.

All good enough reasons, but they were excuses. I felt utterly betrayed, in a daze but trying to stay strong and act the hard man. Putting a brave face on it for Sasha as she would get wild if I acted too sad, but Pepper's betrayal cut deeper than I ever thought it would have.

How could he do that to me?

We'd been buddies for almost three years now, and he'd been an irregular, but mostly welcome, part of my life. I knew he was a man of rather questionable character, but then weren't we all? What I hadn't believed was that he'd betray me. There are criminals, and then there are dirty criminals, and those that would betray their own, their friends, their partners, they were about as unclean as you could get.

We'd done several jobs together, me getting in touch if I needed his help, or him hearing about it and calling me, checking to see if I needed assistance. Before then I'd mostly worked solo, but there was something about the skinny guy I found endearing. We hit it off, in a strange, and yes, maybe often one-sided way. But that's just the way the dice roll sometimes. You have a main guy and you have a sidekick. He gave off that kind of vibe and we fell into our roles easily.

I did jobs, he tagged along. He was one of those characters involved in lots of dodgy dealings in our world. A face. This underground world wasn't large, and the magical underground even smaller, so we all knew each other if not by birthday then at least by name or reputation. What can I say? I liked him.

And he'd planned to screw me over if possible and take the bag and sell it to someone. Meaning, there was somebody out there who really, really wanted it. They'd also got to Boris, so they weren't being subtle. Boris was more of an opportunist and would take anything if he thought he could get away with it, and often even if he wasn't sure.

Now all these guys were dead, my clothes were scorched, wet, and generally messed up, my hat was a little battered after Mike's attempts to take it off my head, and my soul was weeping even if my eyes weren't.

"You coming in? Have a stroll, get some fresh air?" I asked Sasha as she pulled up a discreet distance from my front door like usual. I knew her answer but it was polite to ask.

She turned her nose up and said, "No. Dirty. Why can't you live somewhere clean instead of somewhere so nasty."

I sighed, not in the mood for this argument yet again. "Sasha, my dear godmother, I will be forever grateful to you for the gifts you have bestowed on me, for the help you have just given me and the help you have provided in the past on many occasions, but when will you get it into your thick skull that it's not dirt, it's called the bloody countryside."

There was silence. Terrible, long silence. I braced myself, fearing the worst, and then it happened. Sasha's eyes were wet and I was feeling all kinds of nasty. "There's no need to shout," she croaked, the tears really flowing now.

I pulled a tissue out of the glove box and dabbed at her beautiful, oversized, and peculiarly shaped eyes. Like elongated tear drops, golden and deep, hinting at the magic she contained.

"Sorry, sorry it's been a stressful time lately. Look, I like my home, and it's just the countryside."

"But there's mud," said Sasha, adamant and now beginning to get on my nerves. But she was crying, and I went to pieces when women cried. It's not fair, shouldn't be allowed.

Keeping my calm, knowing it would do neither of us any good to argue, and still grateful for her help, I said, "Thanks for everything. You okay now?"

Sasha sniffed and shook her head, her salon-fresh locks tumbling around her shoulders like liquid gold. I looked away as it never paid to stare at her too long. I got urges, and having urges for your faery godmother feels wrong on so many levels. Motes of faery dust glittered in the interior of the Jeep, fading away before they touched anything.

"I'm okay. Be careful, Arthur, you know what you're like when you get upset. You humans and your deaths. So inconvenient."

"Tell me about it." I leaned over and kissed her lightly on the forehead. My lips tingled and everything felt better in the world for the contact with such a beautiful, otherworldly creature as Sasha, and I guess as I leaned back I had a goofy look on my face.

"Idiot," she said, smiling and batting at me as I held out my hand. She took it anyway, and I gave it a squeeze, her slender fingers easily wrapping around my admittedly rather bony digits.

"Love you," I said, and hopped out.

"Love you, too," she replied, and I know she meant it. "Say hello to George for me, and remind her we're having a girls' day out next week."

"Will do."

I grabbed the bag of mystery, the cause of so much death in such a short time, and closed the door.

Sasha backed away and was gone in a screech of tires.

For a while I was lost deep in thought, and when I came back to myself I was already feeling more relaxed for the change of scene from the city to home. I opened the latch on the four-bar gate and stomped through the cobbled courtyard of my home.

Maybe she was right. It was very muddy.

But this was England, and it was muddy everywhere that wasn't paved over.

May there be more mud and less concrete, that was my motto. Or it would be if I bothered with such things.

I dodged chickens, waved at the sheep—who ignored me as usual—and threw Sally a bucket of scraps which she snuffled then munched on contentedly.

Ah, there's nothing like home, except magic, that's pretty damn cool, too.

"Stupid," I moaned, slamming my palm into my forehead. Why hadn't I asked her what was in the bag? She would have known. Sasha knew everything, and sometimes she even shared that information.

Oh well, time for coffee.

Home

Company is fine and all, in limited doses, but there's nothing like closing the door to your own private world and knowing you're safe. As the door clicked shut with a satisfying *thud, thud, thud,* and I spied the dusty baseball bat in the corner, I felt a sense of comfort that allowed me to relax.

Plus the wards, mustn't forget the wards.

My home of many years was not what many expected, the few that were invited. Some were downright surprised by the way I lived, somehow it seeming at odds—to them—with the way I behaved when in the midst of one underground issue or other.

Screw them. Their loss.

People who spent their whole lives in the city, in concrete jungles where they pounded pavements, lived in sterile interiors, hardly ever spent time in their garden or visited the parks, they were so out of touch with the reality of existence it was no wonder the population was so crazed.

I saw it in their eyes. A madness creeping over them year after year, a tension that would find release in the worst way possible. It was there, the knowledge that something was wrong, a piece missing. Life wasn't quite right but they didn't know what the issue was or what they could do to change things.

I could have told them, but they wouldn't listen, so I kept quiet and left them to it. But one day, one stressful day the same as so many others, somebody would bump into them on a busy street, or someone would cut them off on the road and they'd lose the plot. Tip over the edge and go wild. Rant and rave and react in a way that seemed entirely misplaced, but in reality was the outpouring of tension built over countless years, finally releasing in an explosion of violence, or a complete mental breakdown.

So, yeah, not wanting any of that, I guess you could call me a smallholder. Except I didn't have cows, they were too much trouble and who had the time?

I rose early—if I'd even gone to bed—fed the chickens, collected eggs, tended sheep, even had a donkey named Marjorie. Had pigs, grew my own vegetables, and was mostly self-sufficient in all the basics.

That's not to say I didn't go to the supermarket and buy ice cream or wine, or countless other goodies that made life enjoyable, but most of what I put in my body was organic and home grown.

A wizard needs to look after his health, but that's not really the reason. I needed the connection to the natural world in order to channel magic, and I needed the exercise. Physical exertion on a daily basis to allow me to at least try to sleep at night.

I'd lived in many places and been many people over the years before I finally settled on being the man I should have been all along—no easy thing to find yourself in the modern world. This life, with occasional hard physical labor, was the only way I could get my rest, so important for all things magical.

A true insomniac, if I didn't have all this to keep me busy then I'd be an utter zombie, prowling around all night and half dead. It was bad enough anyway—many nights sleep eluded me completely and in the dark hours I returned to the city, more often than not awake when most others slept.

But not those in my world, they thrived in the quiet hours, under the cover of darkness.

Maybe this was why I was who I was, a criminal, because the underworld worked when the good guys were wrapped up tight in their beds.

But it was damn nice to be home.

My home was large, the property extensive. A proper farm. Animals running about, barns and mud and a massive, ancient building that dated back to the sixteen hundreds in parts, with several additions over the years.

From the outside it was quaint and traditional, on the inside it was slightly different.

It was full of small, comfortable rooms, exposed beams and rough, traditionally lime-plastered walls. Nice, but it always felt like it was missing something and I couldn't relax, felt too claustrophobic.

So after I bought the farm and spent a few years living in the cramped rooms, I had a brainwave one day and got the contractors in.

The end result was a mix of old and new downstairs, while the upstairs remained mostly original. More bedrooms than were needed, two en-suite, and lacking much in the way of modernization. The house was awesome. I did a grand job even if I do say so myself.

Mud and boots stayed outside. Inside was a hodge-podge of crammed bookcases and organized chaos that gave way to spaces almost Shaker-like in their simplicity. I cooked, I cleaned, I relaxed, and I shut out the city for a few blissful hours each and every day.

But sometimes I did what I did best, and that was steal other people's stuff for money. But don't feel bad for them, they deserved it, and I saw this as a life of retirement. I didn't work because I had to, I worked because it was the right thing to do. Okay, you got me. Sometimes it was the right thing, sometimes it was, shall we say, rather debatable.

You wouldn't believe the number of items this world contained that it shouldn't, and you certainly wouldn't believe the badasses that would do anything to get their hands on them. Me included.

Anyway, I was home. Standing with my back to the door, I called out, "You'll never guess what Pepper did. He actually killed me, like, with a knife."

"I told you not to trust him. It's his eyes, too close together," came a voice from the den.

I wandered in and said, "Yes, thank you for that insight, George. Remind me to buy a notepad and pen just so I can write down what is undoubtedly one of the greatest sentences ever uttered."

"Dick," said George, back to scanning her magazine from her position on the sofa.

I loved her to bits, she was my daughter after all, but kids, they drive you nuts.

"Oh, did you get it?" I asked, knowing it would cheer me up and her likewise.

The magazine was put down with a rustle of advert-laden pages and she smiled as she caught my eye. "Yup. Postie came early and I even left the wrapping on." George nodded over at a tightly wrapped cartridge on the coffee table and we shared a moment. Nothing bonds like blasting the hell out of each other, and we'd both become rather addicted to the violent world of two-player shoot-em-ups.

"You wanna unwrap it?" I asked, offering because it was one of her favorite things to do.

George sat up and leaned forward, eyeing the game greedily. "You sure? You love taking off the wrapper."

"Be my guest. As long," I said, a warning in my tone, "as you haven't messed up the kitchen."

"Like I'd dare," she said, knowing it was the one thing she was never to do. She could pile her stuff anywhere, leave her strange, esoteric hair and makeup devices that looked more like torture implements than beauty products, anywhere she liked, but the kitchen had rules. Rules to be obeyed.

"Do I need to check?"

"No!"

"All right then, go for it."

I watched, delighted, as George sprang from the sofa and snatched up the game. She concentrated, tongue sticking out the side of her mouth, as she attacked the wrapping. With expertise that only came from much practice, she teased a corner of the cellophane that had left many mere mortals so frustrated they cried, and in one fluid motion she pulled the end off and slid the game out in a quick stroke.

"Ta-da," she said, smiling.

"Good job," I said, such a simple act making me feel happier than maybe it should. It's the little things in life, and seeing my own flesh and blood happy made me feel like maybe there was some good left in the world. "Set it up and I'll make coffee."

"Roger that."

I left George to it while I went into the kitchen.

The Call

I set things up for coffee, then fished my phone out of a pocket and pulled it from its protective case. I'd learned from too much experience that the damn things broke way too easy so always carried it in what amounted to a miniature safe. Rugged steel housing that could withstand the rigorous life of a wizard in peril.

With a sigh, I tapped in a number I'd called plenty of times before. It was answered on the first ring.

"You weren't there," said Nigel. He did like to state the obvious.

"I know, I was somewhere else instead. I was getting tied up, escaping, running away as cars exploded, then getting tied up again. Oh, and almost murdered, and beaten, and Pepper is dead." I left out the betrayal bit, I couldn't think of that now or I'd never see this day through with the focus I knew it warranted.

"My dear boy, I'm so sorry. This life of intrigue we lead is fraught with hidden dangers. You should be more careful." Nigel always managed to discuss even the most important of topics with a cool detachment that had often made me wonder if he was even capable of emotion.

Maybe it was the upper class, clipped tones, or the fact he had but one position—back ramrod straight, face emotionless, and eyes somehow always distant—or maybe it was his training. Either way, it was creepy. But he was good at his job, and that job was paying me for doing things nobody else could.

"I was trying to be careful. A heads-up about every lowlife knowing about the item and wanting it would have been nice, and could have saved lives."

There was silence for a moment. Nigel was thinking, and when he paused to think I knew he would say nothing good. "Ah, so the word is out. This is unforeseen, most inconvenient."

"Duh! You could've warned me about this beforehand." I scratched at my face in frustration, chin rasping. I needed a shave. It was beyond stylish, verging on wild wizard territory.

"Didn't want to worry you unnecessarily. Now, all this kerfuffle aside, I assume you still have the item?"

Nigel was utterly exasperating at times, but paid well, and his intel was usually spot on, so this wasn't good news. If he hadn't realized word was out then things were very serious. Or, and this may well have been the case, he was lying as usual. I didn't trust him; he was too calm. Never trust somebody that doesn't get emotional, they're hiding something nasty in their closet.

"Yes, I still have it. And what I would like is to not. You ready to go again? Next rendezvous point?" I hated it when I caught myself talking like this. Rendezvous point? Why didn't I just say, meeting place? See the effect he had on me?

"I shall await the pleasure of your company with bated breath." He hung up.

I put my phone back in its case and dropped it into a pocket. The kitchen was full of the beautiful aroma of coffee, so I grabbed the milk, steamed it, sprinkled chocolate dust carefully, and savored a cheeky sip before I took them into the den.

Aah, nothing like it in this world.

Smiling as I drank, I admired a view I could never grow tired of. The sheep nibbled contentedly in the lush, green fields, the trees swayed gently in the wind, and the gray skies were crowded with fat clouds clamoring for position. No matter the weather, it was still beautiful, and how the world should be. Even if for most it couldn't be farther from their reality.

Thoughts of Pepper pushed aside my moment of clarity and it turned everything sour. How could he?

"Lesson learned, Arthur. This is what happens when you let unsavory characters get too close. They hurt you." I should have known by now, but friendship was hard to find let alone hold on to, and I genuinely thought the piece of shit was a buddy.

"Ugh. It's done, you've got new problems to worry about."

Most of the house might be cluttered and in good need of a dust and maybe several skips could be filled with unwanted items, but the kitchen was a different matter entirely.

I liked to cook, and I required order when it counted, and in the kitchen it definitely counted. Everything had its place, and everything was neat and organized. The space was cramped when I bought the farm, even had an old Rayburn stove. But after the first month's bill for the oil it consumed like a hungry beast I got the monster ripped out. It's one thing living in the romantic idyll of a farmhouse, it's another when you realize your stove costs more to run than a car.

In its place I had a snazzy, high-end oven, supposedly self-cleaning although that was a downright lie—it got dirty and cleaning it was one of those jobs I hated with a vengeance. Still, it got scrubbed anyway, same as the rest of the kitchen, and I always left it as I found it. Sparkling, shiny, and smelling of lemon.

This was my real home, the kitchen. And the den. Other downstairs rooms hardly got used. Starting with the old guzzler, I got rather carried away with plumbing and contractors and ended up removing the wall between the kitchen and dining room and knocking the entire back wall of the house down. Steel was inserted where necessary so I didn't end up with just a pile of old rock, and I had floor to ceiling glass doors fitted that looked out onto the fields at the rear. Plus a nice deck for sitting, with a new overhang to allow me to have the space open to the elements without getting soaked.

Instead of the old flagstones that remained everywhere else, I got expensive black porcelain tiles fitted, a modern and sleek kitchen installed with more gadgets than in a Star Trek fan's wet dream, and cupboards, cupboards, everywhere. Although, why you always run out of room however many you have is just one of those kitchen mysteries never to be solved, not even by the most adept of detectives.

A large country table and mismatched chairs with cushions softened the feel of the otherwise clinical room, and the end result was utter, blissful, tranquil, ordered perfection.

With another quick sip of coffee, I wandered back into the den, low-ceilinged and overflowing with stuff, and was greeted with a wall of noise.

I handed George her coffee and with a grunt she clacked a button. I snatched up my controller and battle commenced.

Half an hour later, eyes glazed and mind full of zombie mayhem, I sank the dregs of my cold coffee, said, "Next time I'll whoop your ass," and then ruffled George's hair because I knew she loved it really. "Time to recharge the batteries." As an afterthought, I reminded her, "Don't forget to clean the cups and—"

"I know, and put them back where they belong." George batted my hand away as I went to ruffle her hair again, then smiled at me as I poked my tongue out at her.

"See you soon."

I headed off to the magic room.

The Quiet Place

Most refused to believe in magic, which is understandable considering it was about as common as the Queen playing pool and downing pints of ale at the local on a Friday night.

And yet, anyone could learn a little about this art, could get that incredible buzz of excitement, feel the anticipation build as you get the tingle all over your body and channel unimaginable powers in ways even the most adept cannot explain.

But, as with everything worth having, it came at a price. One most would never be willing to pay even if you sat them down in a comfy chair, gave them irrefutable proof that magic existed, then told them exactly how they too could wield the mystical arts.

It all boiled down to hard work and the ability to stay very still for a very long time.

Think of it like this. A lizard is pretty useless, slow and lethargic, unenergized and good for nothing until it has basked in the sun, soaked up warmth and energy. The longer it exposes itself to the warming and power-giving rays of the sun, the faster it can run, the better its reflexes, and the more likely it is to feed successfully and thus do the same thing all over again the next day.

Or here's another example. Batteries. We all know what they are. They have to be charged. Say a big ole battery, those you use to go camping with, is dead, expunged. You connect your solar panel and wait patiently for it to charge up. If the sun is weak because it's cloudy, then it takes longer to charge, same as the lizard. But if the sky is clear, blue and beautiful—which didn't happen often in the UK so good job I wasn't a lizard—then that means the connection to the power source is better and before you know it, whoopee, you've plugged in your power-hungry link to the online world and away you go.

Magic's like that.

When you are still, when you can calm your mind and let it rest in the Quiet Place, the emptiness that is both within and without—which I know sounds all spiritual and a little like I'm trying to get you to take up meditation or become the Buddha, but what can I tell you, it's a big universe out there and this stuff is important—then you can maybe, just maybe, search and eventually find the connection. The power source, the unknowable, impossible to describe, mighty, all-encompassing energy source of the entire universe.

It's what powers your mind, what makes the planets rotate and stops everything imploding, or never existing in the first place. The driving force behind the whole shebang, existence itself. God to some, nirvana to billions, some science thing to do with atomic particles to others. It doesn't matter what you call it as you will never even come close to the truth of the nature of this thing, but what you can call it, and what we did, those of us who went to the Quiet Place, is magic.

That's what everyone calls stuff they don't understand, right? Magic.

Spend time there, silent, mind empty of everything but the desire, the need, the will to open yourself to such primordial forces, and you get a tiny taste of it inside of you.

And just like batteries, and lizards, you top yourself up when you run down to almost empty.

What I'm trying to tell you, what this all equates to, is it's damn hard to even get to this place. I mean, who is ever still, alone, mindful of their thoughts, and focused on nothing? Right. And if you want to direct these forces then you need hours to make the connection, more if you are really low on your levels, and it may take you years to find the Quiet Place, let alone understand how to take what it offers.

And that, my friend, was why nobody believed in magic and why there weren't that many people in the world who could use it.

It took too much damn hard work for anyone to bother looking, let alone find out what they could do with it. Plus, there was TV. Oh, and the Internet, that was good, too.

And let's not forget gaming.

Back at It

After the morning I'd had, I could have done with more than half an hour in the magic room but it would have to do. I wasn't exactly topped up to the max but at least I wasn't just a mere mortal either.

I call it the magic room when really it was just an empty room at the top of the house up a narrow set of stairs. Yeah, the attic. It had a single, small, north-facing window, stripped floorboards, bare plastered walls and nothing else.

No distractions, no furniture, nothing but a light bulb and me when I was in it.

Stripped down, ignoring the cold, I sat or sometimes lay and allowed the impossible to happen.

My internal buzzers went off after thirty minutes, so I rose and went into my bedroom to dress. I'd already showered as feeling clean before entering the room had become part of the ritual, not that it made a difference but there you go.

With new black combats on, a fresh brown shirt, Grace on my head, and boots downstairs, I was almost ready to go.

George was still hard at the game as I entered the living room, getting practice in so she could continue to beat me. "Gotta go see a man about a dog," I said.

"Why don't you just say you have to go see Nigel to unload your cursed bag?" she said, not taking her eyes off the screen.

"Because that makes it sound scary, and I don't want you to worry about me."

George paused the game and turned. "I worry more when you don't tell me what's happening. One of these days you know you're going to have to take me with you, right?"

"Never," I said, and I meant it. "You're my responsibility and this life isn't for you. You're safe here, it's off limits and protected, but out there, it's a different matter entirely."

"Come on, Arthur, I mean, Dad, you know I'm ready." It was only recently she'd started calling me Dad and she was still getting used to it, me too, so slipped sometimes. Still, it was nice to hear when she remembered. It made my heart sing like nothing else, even better than magic.

"You'll be ready when I'm dead and cremated, and not before."

"Spoilsport." George resumed her game. Guess the conversation was over.

"Bye, then," I said, hoping for a hug and a kiss goodbye but knowing she wasn't ready for anything like that yet.

"Laters," was all I got, and the back of her hand before it slammed onto the controller and she hissed, "Yes!" as pixelated blood splattered the screen.

I put my boots on at the front door and wandered through the courtyard. Footsteps pounded behind me and I turned.

"Thought maybe you'd want to take this?" George held out the bag and tutted as I took it.

"Thanks. Oh, and thanks for sorting the animals out this morning. Any problems?"

"Nope, just don't make a habit of it. I'm a teenager, we aren't supposed to get up before eleven."

"I won't. And thanks again for the bag."

George smiled and I took a moment to study my daughter. She was a pretty girl, rich auburn hair down her back she played with constantly. Subtle makeup when she could be bothered, but always smartly dressed. She went against everything I thought I knew about teenagers. She didn't rebel with her wardrobe, liked tight pastel skirts and frilly, button down blouses, so maybe she was like an anti-rebel rebel or something. Not sure, it got confusing. But, she rebelled in other ways, magical ways, and however much I tried to talk her out of it, she carried on regardless.

"Stop staring at me," she said, blushing a little.

"Sorry, just thinking how pretty you are."

"Dad!"

"What?

"Ugh, you're so weird. How the hell you're a good criminal is beyond me," she said, then ran back inside.

"I'll have you know I'm the best there is," I shouted. She just slammed the door and made the chickens squawk. I glared at them and mumbled, "Can't help it if I forget things now and then. I've got stuff on my mind."

I opened the gate and got in my car, no point using a "borrow" now. The job was done and besides, I needed a ride I was familiar with in case things got hairy now word was apparently out about the item.

Mindful of wayward magic and the fact the item clearly didn't like being manhandled and had a penchant for causing cars to explode, I activated the wards now we were out the house—I knew George was nosy and didn't want her arm melting off; I'd never hear the end of it—then topped them up and placed the bag carefully on the back seat.

Sitting behind the wheel, I adjusted my hat, running my fingers around the brim in a way that calmed and comforted me, the soft material as familiar as my own fingers.

You may think it strange that I hadn't been tempted to look inside the duffel to see what all the fuss was about, but secrecy was something I was used to. I had discovered, at much personal peril and not a little pain over the years, that often knowing as little as possible was an excellent idea.

Whatever was inside wouldn't change the fact I had to follow through on my job, and knowing just by sending out feelers to the item that it was well-guarded and made my wards look like those of an amateur, told me all I needed to know. Take a peek and it could be curtains, and there was another reason, too.

I could sense something.

It was guarded, almost as if sleeping and dreaming deeply. There was a presence, not evil, not kind, a neutral sentience way beyond anything I wanted to awaken, and I knew with absolute certainty that if I opened the bag it would allow someone to see me, to know me, and the thing inside would awaken. I was unsure what that meant, but understood it would be nothing that would make my life more complete.

So, sensible lad that I was, I didn't even think about peeking.

Haha, believe that and you'll believe anything.

Of course I was dying to look, but I still knew it was one hell of a bad idea.

"To the city," I ordered my car, but, as usual, it remained silent and I had to do all the driving myself. You'd think living in the 21st century would mean there were proper cool cars by now but no, same old, same old.

I crunched the old girl into first, eased off slowly so I didn't get caught in a rut, and headed into the city to meet Nigel.

With any luck I'd be on my way home in an hour or so with my payment and feeling a lot lighter of spirit.

Guess what happened?

No, I wasn't surprised either.

An Interruption

There was a rule, unwritten as all the best ones are. Actually, there were lots of rules the supernatural, and just downright criminal elements I mixed in abided by come hell or high water.

One of the most important was that family and loved ones remained untouchable. If you weren't directly in the life then you were invisible. You didn't exist in our world. You may be the wife of a gangster, a girlfriend, casual acquaintance, or a son or daughter. You were never fair game, you didn't exist.

We could beat the crap out of each other, could maim, kill, double-cross, kidnap, any of it, we'd made our choice and knew the score, but that's as far as it went.

Even so, I had ensured my home was protected with the strongest magic I could summon but Sasha still laughed at me when she came to my home for the first time. She beefed up the security with true, otherworldly magic, and I'd maybe not slept better but at least lay with my eyes open through the night a lot more peacefully ever since.

Even if somebody wanted to get inside, or some thing, because, let's face it, the beasties couldn't care less about the games of humans, they would find it impossible. The place was a fortress.

That didn't stop me picking up my phone and tapping my foot impatiently as I waited for my call to be answered just moments after I came to a stop in the road less than a quarter mile from home.

"Hello?" said George, clearly distracted as I could hear the sound of heavy machine gun fire blaring from the TV.

"Bunker time," I said.

"Again? You're way too paranoid," she said, not taking it seriously.

"Only because they really are out to get me. No arguments, go now. Take the game with you."

"Fine," she said. "Ah, shit, you scumbag."

"George? George? Hello? Are you okay?"

The line went dead.

Action Stations

The sound of Dre filled the car a moment later. My phone ringing. What can I tell you, I like rap.

"Sorry, got distracted and tapped the screen by mistake."

"You gave me a bloody heart attack."

"Should I call for an ambulance?" asked George, sounding worried.

"No. I don't mean a literal one, I mean... Look, forget it. Get into the bunker, this is no joke. In fact, spend the day there. Go nuts and eat the ice cream, whatever you want. Take the game and stay there until I come home. Okay?"

"Fine, but I'm warning you, if you forget to call again and I end up down there for days getting worried, I'll eat it all and then I'll be so fat you'll never get me out."

"Haha, there's nothing to you, just skin and bone. Sorry." Lame, I know, but I'd become cautious and over-protective since George came into my life.

"Gotta stay slim so I can binge when I'm locked in basements."

"It's not a basement, it's a bunker. You know, like a panic room. Only, um, don't panic in there, just enjoy yourself."

"Oh, I'm sure I will. Not. What's happening? Anything I should be concerned about?"

I eyed the car blocking my path and replied, "No, just a chancer, but better safe than sorry. I should have said before I left."

"Okay, see ya later," said George, sounding chipper and I knew thinking of ice cream already.

"See you—" *Click.* She'd hung up. "Later."

I stuffed my phone back into my pocket, patted my right thigh and felt the comforting wood—hey, you know what I mean—and then sat. Waiting.

George was seventeen, going on seventy, going on seven. She morphed between moody teenager, a child unable to perform the simplest of tasks, and a whirlwind of bossiness. Offering an avalanche of instruction on how I should live my life. She could go days without getting dressed, would sometimes become manic and clean the house in a disturbing frenzy of activity, and had been found prone on the floor kicking her feet and banging her fists whilst weeping uncontrollably because she couldn't figure out how to get her admittedly less than impressive wand to change color and sparkle like Sasha's.

Apparently, this was what most teenage girls were like. I had this on good authority from George herself, and I guess she was in the best position to know. All I remember about seventeen-year-old girls is that when I was their age they wouldn't let me anywhere near them, they smelled nice if I did somehow get close enough, and they sure as hell never hid in underground, magically shrouded bunkers. Unless I was very out-of-touch, and that's entirely possible.

Still, George was no regular kid, and she hadn't had a regular upbringing from what I could tell.

I was a rather bewildered single father, and it still sounds weird to say that word.

Father.

It was all rather sudden. One day I was at home wandering around in my boxers, drinking coffee, the next there was a knock at the door and I had to wear clothes inside the house.

"You're my father," said the soaked thing on my doorstep. "Your wards are crap. I could come in no problem if I wanted to," were the words my daughter used to introduce herself into my world.

"I guess that makes you my daughter, then. But no way could you break the wards," I said, calm on the outside but panicking so much on the inside I had to suck in my belly so it didn't wobble.

"No, wait!" I shouted, but she stepped off the mat and her foot hovered in the air just inside the doorway as her body went rigid and her face froze in a rictus of pain. Tears fell and even as I lowered the wards she was flung backward and landed in the mud.

It took her a week to recover, and in that time I got the whole sorry story.

"Eh?" My daydreaming about George was interrupted by a rap on the window.

"We gonna do this, or not?" asked a handsome man with a jawline to die for, wearing a black designer t-shirt, limbs tight with scrawny muscles and popping veins.

"I'd rather we didn't," I said. "I've got somewhere to be."

"And I've got this," he said, raising his right hand and placing the muzzle of a gun against the window pane.

"Ooh, got one for me?"

"Just get out, wizard," he said, sneering in a way he obviously practiced in front of a mirror. "And don't try anything. You may be fast, but you aren't this fast." He pointed at the gun with his free hand.

He had a point.

A Tall, Dark Stranger

I got out of the car slowly, the man's gun trained on me. "Move to the front," he ordered.

Making no sudden movements, I did as I was told like a good wizard and asked, "What can I do for you? Are you sure you have the right wizard? There are a lot of us about, you know. Quite common nowadays."

"Shut up. Where is it?" He glanced inside the car and spotted the duffel on the back seat. "That it?"

"No. It's another nice duffel, not the one you're after at all."

"They said you thought you were funny. They also said you were a wizard. Haha, a wizard. These guys, they crack me up." To be honest, he didn't look particularly amused, and he didn't look like he believed it either, which was good.

"Is that a wand in your pocket, or are you just pleased to see me?" he said, cracking a smile and chuckling at his own joke.

"Haha, like I haven't heard that one before."

"Just empty your pockets. Hurry up, I don't got all day."

"Don't have. It's don't have," I said, ripping open the Velcro—it's good for a fast draw.

"Just do it!" The smile faded and the stony stare returned.

I'd met this kind of killer countless times and they were all pretty much the same. They didn't care about human life and they didn't even care about themselves. They lived only for the thrill and for the fear they could instill in others. But he was getting jittery and trigger-happy already as I wasn't acting scared or doing what he thought I should.

I pulled the wand out my pocket and said, "Now what?"

"What the hell? It really is a wand! Why the fuck do you have a stick in your pocket? You don't actually believe you're a wizard do you? Like, for real?"

In answer, I moved my hands like you do in conversation, the utter incompetent not for one minute thinking I could do anything with it. As my focus and charge drew down into the wand and the expertly carved sigils running down the shaft glowed deep, burnished orange against the dark wood, my aim was spot on. A jolt of invisible energy slammed into his radius, breaking the bone. The gun dropped, his hand was left hanging limp, and he screamed.

"Amateur," I said as I blew on the end of my wand and holstered it. Okay, pocketed it, but you know what I mean.

"You broke my arm," the guy wailed. He cradled it with his other hand and screamed loudly as the bone snapped again, the magic having worked as directed. I could have done without the draining, but needs must and all that.

"Of course I broke your arm, you had a gun on me."

"I'll kill you for this," he hissed, his forehead already slick with sweat from the pain.

"Tell you what," I said, "how about we both go our merry ways and pretend this never happened?"

"No way. I'm gonna..."

Man, this guy was predictable. I could see his mind working, thinking he'd distract me while he grabbed the gun from the road while we talked. I stepped forward and as he bent I put a well-worn sole over his good hand, grabbed the broken arm, and squeezed. Tight. As he screamed, I looked him in the eye and said, "Don't test me. I'm having a bad day."

His body relaxed a little so I removed my foot. "Back up." As he did, I picked up the gun and then emptied out the bullets, wiped it clean, and threw it into the brook beside the road.

"I'll put this down to you being an utter fuckwit and I'll be on my way now. You don't even have to tell me who sent you as I'm not someone who goes in for torture and I doubt you'll talk otherwise. But be warned. I never want to see you again. Do you understand me?"

"Yeah. Whatever."

"Good. Nice t-shirt by the way."

I left him there and got back into my car.

Some people, they just never knew when to admit they were beaten. Before I started the car, he drew on his bravado and shouted, "I know where you live. Hear you've got a young girl in there." He smirked, then winced with pain, and began walking to his vehicle.

I yanked open the car door, my anger bubbling over, and by the time I got to him my wand was in my hand, gripped so tight the spell-infused symbols that came to life at my touch were already burning into my palm.

"What the fuck did you say? You are one utter piece of shit, you know that?"

"Shut up, old man. You won, for now." He moved to open his car door but I slammed it shut again and faced him square on.

"What, you gonna blast me with your stick again? Pathetic. It's just some stupid new stunner or something. You're like a child, pretending to be a wizard."

"No, I need to conserve my energy for those that are actually a problem. And you, you filth, are no longer a problem."

Sticks, wands, staffs, rods, whatever you want to call them, magical or otherwise, are excellent weapons in their own right. They are, after all, long, hard, and easy to wield. Why do you think almost every police force in the world has some form of truncheon, baton, or similar? Because they're effective, that's why.

Adjusting my grip with expert timing from countless hours of practice, I held my wand like a javelin and thrust it with all my strength into his right eye.

It sank halfway up the shaft and only stopped when it hit bone. I ripped it out with a gross sucking sound and pushed the man over before bending and wiping the wood clean on his t-shirt.

"Nobody threatens my daughter. Nobody. There are rules."

My heart raced and adrenaline surged. It's scary, these things we are capable of, but I would not stand for anyone stepping over the line most of us wouldn't dream of crossing. I'd met some of the nastiest, cruelest, meanest men to have ever existed, preternatural creatures too, and they would never dream of making a threat like this dude had. It was about respecting the boundaries we'd set ourselves, and if you crossed them then you got what you deserved.

I pulled out my phone. "All clear," I said, then hung up as George began shouting at the TV screen.

I made another call, this one to the best cleaner in town, and gave instructions.

Then I dragged the body to the car, bundled him inside, parked it in a verge not far away and walked back to mine.

With my body back under control but my mood a little darker, I continued my drive into the city.

I wanted rid of this damn bag, and the sooner the better.

An Appointment

Time is fluid. When you sit staring at a clock it moves slower than when you are engrossed in a good book or shooting up bad guys in a computer game—or real life.

Some will argue that time is just time, it doesn't move faster or slower. Nonsense. Of course it does. It's a measurement of the ever-changing present, as you can only exist in the present, never the past or future, and everyone's perception of time is different, depending on what it is they are doing and how their body reacts to said situation.

Nigel didn't see it like that.

For my broker, although that's a rather narrow definition of what he was and what he did, time was one thing, and one thing only—a measure of the man.

He was a stickler for punctuality, adhered to it rigidly, and expected others to do likewise. Nigel was never late or early, and if you failed to turn up when arranged you'd find him gone, or leaving. He was also keen on giving you a look. A weighing up of you as a person, concluding that you must be lacking if you couldn't even perform such a simple task as keeping an appointment.

It was fair enough. In our world time often became crucial. Miss your moment, fail to take advantage of an opportunity when it arose and act with split-second accuracy and you may have blown not only your chance of getting paid but you could very well forfeit your life, too.

So I arrived early.

Truth be told, I was not in the best of moods now. What with the morning I'd had and the death of Pepper, I was shaken, even if my demeanor didn't show the frail state I was in. My body ached something terrible from the beating, and although the pain was fading thanks to the energy within, it would take time for me to feel one hundred percent again. Plus, my nose kept grinding, which was disconcerting, and it kept making a weird whistling noise, which was downright embarrassing.

A few bruises were the least of my worries, though. I was more concerned about the mess Nigel had got me into. It was unheard of for people like the man I'd killed to come after magical artifacts, it just wasn't how things worked. These type of objects of power and immense curiosity were true underground stuff, the realm of the magical only. Nobody in that circle would send somebody who didn't even believe in magic to try to retrieve it, so something was very amiss.

Was it just a chancer? Somebody who'd heard something somehow and sent a hired assassin to get what they believed to be merely valuable? It was the logical explanation and that meant it was probably the truth, but it didn't bode well at all for me if every Tom, Dick, and Harry in the underground knew The Hat had something precious.

My guess was it was something to do with Boris. One of his goons must have talked and word spread. Much of the criminal activity in the UK had nothing to do with magic, and quite a lot of the jobs I'd done were carried out with small groups of men and women who wouldn't believe I was a wizard if I waved my wand and turned them into frogs.

Sure, everyone knew the rumors and the aura of mystique around people like myself, but they didn't actually believe. It wasn't a part of everyday life no matter if you were a criminal or perfectly respectable. If something weird happens, if things occur that you cannot explain then you don't just suddenly believe it must be magic, you conclude it was just one of those strange, inexplicable things and get on with your day.

So chances were good that the idiot I'd dealt with earlier was a cheap killer-for-hire sent by an opportunist who knew better than to mess with me directly.

It wasn't the case that everyone feared me, they certainly didn't, but many respected me or at least didn't actively despise me, anyway. The Hat was a face. One of the best, and they knew that. I dealt with top-tier operatives only. Worked only with the best, and then only if absolutely necessary, as, let's be honest, they were a bunch of criminals and I wouldn't trust them with my toothbrush let alone anything valuable.

And that's just the general gangsters.

The supernatural world I spent the majority of time in was a different beast entirely.

There everyone knew who and what I was, and to some extent what I could do and the work I got involved in. They also knew I had close links to Nigel, and for all his faults, Nigel commanded respect from everyone. Everyone.

He had something about him that made you question the facade he presented. There was an awful lot more going on beneath the surface than met the eye. He was too quietly confident about everything. The most self-assured person I'd ever met, and I'd met some seriously cocky buggers in my time. Nigel's breeding wasn't just a screen to hide behind, he truly was the epitome of upper-class British stoicism and made no apologies for it. Other people from privileged backgrounds tried to play it down, change their accent and their demeanor, stay quiet about their education and knowledge of the world, pretend like they were just another working class Joe.

Not Nigel. He was comfortable in his own skin, fully aware of the image he presented and played on it. Maybe hammed it up would be more accurate. He made no apology for being well-educated and comfortably wealthy. He prided himself on his clipped accent and his even closer clipped blond mustache, and was an entirely respectable gentleman of maybe mid-forties, although that's debatable.

He was also utterly ruthless and would kill you without batting an eyelid if you ever even thought of crossing him. I'd heard the stories, and I'd also seen him in action. He clearly had a military background, and I don't mean as a foot soldier. He would have been high ranking, in charge. The guy was born to boss others around.

Nigel was also a plain human. He'd never dabbled with magic beyond the most basic of basics, and had no interest in furthering esoteric skills. His interest in magic was different to mine, and there were plenty of men and women like him out there.

They understood the power that was there to be tapped into, and often reveled in the magic objects and creatures could give, or contained, but never focused on becoming someone who could control primordial forces through the sheer power of their own will.

Collectors, in other words.

Or, in Nigel's case, a broker of said collectibles of the rather esoteric and extremely rare kind.

A cold-blooded killer who, as far as I could tell, was bereft of most human emotions.

Nigel was a psychopath. And here he was, walking toward me, looking out-of-place amongst the hipsters at the outdoor cafe that thankfully had a large overhang, as, typically, it was raining.

Nigel's face was neutral as he walked neither fast nor slow through the thinning throng of shoppers. He somehow managed to make his black umbrella graceful, bending it this way and that to avoid the people, like a ballerina. He wore his usual tweed three-piece suit and tan, British hand-crafted shoes polished to within an inch of their life—you can bet he didn't do them himself.

His tie was straight, his shirt starched, and his blond hair styled yet unruly in that way many upper-class men seemed to somehow pull off but the youngsters couldn't. He was tall, maybe six-three, slender but hinting at lithe power and speed, and had the bearing of a military man through and through.

From things he's said over the years, and the people he'd put me in contact with when needed, there was no doubt he'd progressed from the military to more covert government work. Whether that was CIA, Special Branch, or something I'd never heard of I truly didn't know, but he knew people, and I wouldn't have been surprised to discover he held a high position in whatever secret organization he was a part of, maybe even ran.

"You're early," he said, nodding at my half-finished coffee which I'd given up on as it was utter crap.

"And you gave me a bouncer."

"My dear fellow, I don't know what you are talking about. I gave you a perfectly legitimate illegal and dangerous assignment to carry out. One you had a very specific payment request for, I might add. Nothing out of the ordinary about it at all."

"Okay, if that's the case answer me this. Why is Pepper dead after trying to take it from me? Why was Boris after it, also dead, and why did some dude stop me by my house and threaten George? My house! Nobody knows about my house, Nigel, you know that."

His eyes grew wide at that, and angry, and you didn't want to mess with Nigel when he was angry. "And why the hell do I get the feeling this thing in the bag is watching me? Oh, and it glows, and blows things up, too."

"Is that it?" he asked, indicating the bag with the slightest nod of his head.

"Duh. I'm not letting it out of my sight until I get what I'm due. And I want it now."

"Hmm, this is rather unexpected, I have to say. Have you looked inside?"

"Seriously? You need to ask? I just want it gone. Now."

"Then allow me to do the honors," Nigel said, and indicated the bag on the chair next to me. He looked curious, almost eager, and usually he was all business, treating the items I got for him as nothing more than simple business transactions. Never showing the slightest hint of whether it was something he personally wanted or merely for a client.

He'd told me this was for a client, though, and that's a rare piece of information coming from him.

Things were not as they seemed. I saw the twitch at the corner of his eye just as my hand closed around the bag's soft leather handle. I paused, watching the tic, but then it stopped.

"Who's it for? You sure it's not just for you?" I asked, hand wrapped tight around the handle but the bag still on the chair.

"For a client. I told you." His lips parted slightly and I caught a glimpse of his wet, pink tongue licking the back of his teeth. He was excited, and nervous.

If you knew Nigel then you knew he didn't do nervous. He was as cool as a corpse in a freezer and a lot less emotional.

My Spidey senses tingled, a feeling I knew better than to ignore. I scanned the street, knowing he had men watching in case of anything unforeseen going down, but I'd already spotted them as he used the same people. No, I was searching for the men he had that he didn't want me to see.

"You motherfucker," I said. "Who are the shifters? You don't deal with those guys. Your goons are always professional. Trained bodyguards, not Wild Ones."

"The Wild Ones are sometimes necessary when I hear of trouble brewing. It takes a monster to catch a monster," he said, voice as calm and casual as if we were chatting about the weather. "And there is no need for bad language, Arthur, I'm your friend."

"That's what I thought, but something's off. See ya." I rose and grabbed the bag, but Nigel was up and beside me in an instant, hand over mine on the bag.

"We had a deal. You do not cross me. You will have your payment, you have what I requested, let's leave it at that."

I focused with wizardly cool while he spoke words I'd expected to hear, and his eyes told a different story. Something was definitely wrong. I saw him think for a moment, as if coming to a conclusion part of him was loathe to accept.

"Run," he whispered so quietly it took a moment for the words to filter through.

I nodded, moving my head a fraction, more passing between us in those few moments than I think it had ever done before. We were friends. He wasn't betraying me, not really. Something was going on, something I didn't know about. He wanted this to be over, too. He just wanted this dealt with and for us to both go on with our lives.

For the first time ever, Nigel was out of his depth.

Then his head exploded in a mass of blood and gore and I did as he'd said.

I ran.

Underground, Overground

There's nothing like seeing the face of somebody you kind of care about explode in front of you to make you reevaluate your life choices. As I scarpered down an alley to the sound of screams and upturned tables and smashed mugs full of revolting, overpriced coffee, I had an epiphany.

No more mystery items.

It may seem strange that I'm not spouting off about the career path I'd chosen, but that would be stupid, and pointless. Do you know how hard it is to go straight after spending a lifetime being involved with this stuff?

No, neither do I.

The absolute worst time to decide to hang up the wand and go play video games all day is when peeps are out to get you, especially peeps with guns who aren't afraid to blast holes in probably the most influential man in the country, give or take a few shadowy figures.

Nigel was a serious player, and these guys clearly weren't afraid of either him, those he served and dealt with, or the authorities.

The bag was playing up as I ran and shouted, "Excuse me," repeatedly before barging past people and generally being a menace to society. It was glowing with what I can only describe as anger. The item did not want to be taken by whoever these characters were, and so far I couldn't blame it.

"I don't know what you are," I said to the bag, "but I wish people would stop dying because of you." No answer.

I turned a sharp left and lost my bearings for a moment, then knew where to go. I had to get to my car, get in it, and drive away very fast. Only problem being, I was heading the wrong way and didn't feel like turning around.

There was a commotion behind me and I knew it wasn't anyone looking for a truce. I couldn't do anything here, couldn't risk it. One of the Laws strictly imposed by the Alliance, part of the Code, was you did not, ever, under forfeit of death in nasty ways, use magic out in the open where it could be witnessed by the general populace. One on one, or even if there were a few unknowing folk, that's one thing, but in crowds, absolutely not. There'd be too many questions, and apart from that, if I managed to get away I'd be hounded by the insufferable Alliance until they found me and did gross stuff.

So my only option was to get away.

Moving fast through the throngs of shoppers, I found myself yanked hard by my free arm and pulled into a doorway. Ready to risk the wrath of the wizards, I moved for my wand but a thick hand clamped down tight and hard.

"I'm saving you, wizard. This way if you wanna live." The Wild One squinted at me with intense eyes.

"Um, you sure you don't wanna kill me?" I asked warily, flustered and not my usual insightful self.

"In there, through the back. Now," he ordered, and shoved me through the front door of a bakery. He was right behind me and grabbed my arm again, nodded to the pink-faced man behind the counter setting out loaves on the display, and then we went through a side door, down a narrow corridor made even narrower by all the proofing loaves, and then into the kitchen proper. A vast space with massive walk in ovens, racks of bread, men rolling loaves and buns, and boy did it smell good.

Guess people ate a lot of bread in this city. I tried to limit carb intake but was willing to have a cheat day.

Maybe another time, as the hairy dude dragged me through and then out the back into a walled courtyard full of plastic trays and industrial bins that would be wheeled out the large gates to the alley beyond.

One thing I'd learned over the years was not to trust shifters. The Wild Ones, as they liked to be known for reasons that will become more than apparent, were about as trustworthy as a cat with a mouse locked in a room and told to play nice.

They were mercenary, cruel, crazed, and dangerous. If that sounds anything like yours truly then tough, but I had a wand and I didn't go around eviscerating people that looked at me funny. Not often, anyway.

Speaking of wands...

Shredded Abs

"Don't touch me again. Who the hell are you? What do you want? Were you working for Nigel?" Yes, I was rambling, but it had been a stressful day. I gripped my wand tight and pointed it right at him, tip blazing hot and ready to shoot... Look, can we stop with this? It's a wand okay? Nothing phallic about it. Okay, there is, but please, this is a serious business.

So, I pointed my wand, my potent energy ready to blast him through the wall if he tried anything. They may have been paid by Nigel, but Nigel was dead, so with it their duty to do what he'd paid them to do.

"All right, mate, don't get your knickers in a twist. You're The Hat, right? Arthur?"

"Yeah," I said warily.

"Heard all about you, innit?"

"Innit? Innit what? What are you talking about?"

"Just a figure of speech, mate, just how I talk." He had a strange lilt to his voice, almost singsong in a gruff old banjo player kind of way. A twang, melodious but very street, if that's the term the kids were using now, which I doubted. I'd have to ask George, assuming I didn't get eaten or shot or something way more inventive in the meantime.

I needed time to think. How the hell had they done this to Nigel? More to the point, why had he got shifters involved? Nigel was old school in so many ways and this wasn't his style at all.

What should I do? Was this guy on the level? Should I tickle the wand to life then do a runner? Or was I overreacting?

He waited patiently while these thoughts and thousands more went through my mind. Something about him made me think he was legit, but I'd been wrong before. Just once or twice.

"Look, dude, it's best if we don't hang around here too long. Nigel has just been pretty effectively shot through the fucking head." He folded his arms across his slender but well muscled chest and tapped his foot impatiently, even though I got the impression he would've waited while we were stormed by whoever shot Nigel and was now after us.

Not us. Me. Not even me. The item.

Mind made up, I said, "Okay, let's go. But this doesn't mean I haven't got a lot of questions for you, buddy. Don't know why this is going to the dogs, er, excuse the idiom, so quickly, and I sure as hell don't know what you and your mates are doing involved in this, but I guess I'll find out as long as I stay alive."

"That's the spirit," he said brightly, well-groomed brown beard shining in the weak light. Damn, but what was with these hipsters? A beard should be ragged and bristly, not looking like it had product in it. I bet he used a comb on it, and that's not right, not in my world.

Dealing with shifters was always a stressful business. You never knew what the hell they'd do next. You could guarantee that nine times out of ten it would come as a shock. One moment you're chatting, or arguing, with a well-manicured man or woman, and the next they're pulling off a dress, unzipping their fly, or generally in a state of undress before their body cracks and pops and they're at your throat.

It was the incongruity of it all that freaked you out the most. They always seemed so smart and respectable, in a casual way. Self-assured with well-toned muscles any gym goer would be proud of—not that I was jealous or anything. The latest fad in the shifter community was for the men to appear coiffed to within an inch of their lives. Strange, otherworldly hairstyles but clearly meant to look like that. The women were just the same.

The Wild Ones' clothes had always been smart bordering on funereal. Maybe it was because of their rebellious nature, refusing to live up to the stereotype the name suggests, not wanting to appear like the animals they truly were. The animal within was never far from the surface, clawing at their insides, them taking years to master the inner demon that would spring free at any moment if their control wavered or faltered.

That's the one thing about the Wild Ones you had to respect no matter what you thought of them as a race, species, or somehow maladjusted human. Yeah, okay, maybe I'm going a little overboard. They were human, but had something inside seriously wonky. DNA corrupted in ways nobody ever came close to explaining.

It was only when you got very near to a shifter you got a sense of their true nature. Animal magnetism drew you close, pulled you in. Over the years, I'd seen it time and time again—people overcome with urges, body almost out of control as they reached out a hand, took a step closer before they even knew what they were doing. You couldn't blame the shifters for that, they weren't responsible for the actions of others, but it didn't take away from the fact they enjoyed it, played on it. They had a scent, a musk, pheromones that made them almost irresistible to members of the opposite sex and just as irresistible to those of the same sex who had even a passing interest in exploring the body of a virile looking member of a very dangerous breed of human.

"Um, look here, mate, you may be The Hat, and I'm sure you've got some wicked skills with that wand of yours," the shifter gave a sly grin but unfortunately for him I wasn't that way inclined, "but can we, like, go do this somewhere we're a little less likely to get our heads shot the fuck off?"

I had a few options, none of them particularly inviting. Either go my own merry way, hope the shifter didn't try to stop me, and deal with whoever it was had just shot Nigel and was after me, or trust that Nigel had known what he was doing when he picked the shifters to protect him. That was the real rub, though, wasn't it? They'd done a piss-poor job of it so far, what with

Nigel's brains now residing in a cup of overpriced, watery, cold coffee.

"Let's go," I said, knowing there was zero chance of this going well.

A Really Wild One

"Hey, what's your name?"

"Wondered when you'd get around to asking. Steve. The name's Steve." He held out a lean, powerful hand. We shook.

"Damn, dude, that's one hell of a grip you got there." Steve looked powerful, but Steve was a lot more powerful than he looked. As we shook, our eyes met, and understanding passed between us. He wouldn't take any of my usual crap—that's what he was telling me.

"Not too shabby yourself, mate," said Steve.

Shifters were hard to read. They didn't go out of their way to advertise their nature, and even when you got to know them well it was still never a simple thing to anticipate what they'd do next. They battled constantly with their inner demons, some hating what they were, others loving it. Reveling in the power inside and itching for the chance to go feral.

"Right, mate," said Steve, "you ready to do this?"

"I'm not exactly sure what this is. What do you have in mind? You guys didn't exactly do a good job protecting Nigel." Steve's lip turned up at the corner in a snarl, and his muscles bunched beneath a shirt that must've taken hours to iron so smooth.

"Hey, you should be thanking me. Nigel said the assignment was probably dangerous, but he didn't say nothing about people coming to blow his fucking head off. Bad news, innit?"

Steve was getting antsy, clearly keen to leave. Me too. I needed time to think not just about my current situation, and how the hell we were going to get away from here, but about the bag and whatever it contained.

How in Buster's name was I supposed to unload this now? Plus, and just as important if not more so, how was I supposed to get paid?

The back door to the bakery crashed open, making us both jump. On autopilot, without consciously thinking of it, my wand was in my hand, energy already spiraling through my system, gathering momentum as it funneled down my arm and the burnished sigils in the wood danced with life.

Beside me, Steve was making weird noises like when you rip the thigh off a chicken, bones and gristle crunching in all kinds of nasty ways. I could see the metamorphosis begin, as surprised as always at the speed, the ferocity, the intensity, the downright nastiness of the whole shifter thing.

Rather him than me. I'd stick to the wand, thank you very much.

Chased

Steve's brown canvas backpack fell from his shoulders and his clothes followed right after. His shirt split and his trousers the same, and it was obvious why he favored lightweight cotton over heavy denim or leather, same as all shifters. They weren't big bikers that's for sure. Can you imagine your body changing shape while you have to try to contend with a leather jacket or thick boots?

An obvious army type didn't even pause as he crashed through the door, gun raised and already firing. I dodged behind the large bin and shouted, "Hurry up," to Steve, but it was already too late.

I pulled back on the lid of the bin and dragged it back to cover me as I headed for the gates. Steve was no longer the smart, confident man I'd just met. He was a large, I mean way too large, and they're big buggers anyway, badger. I know, right?

"A badger? You've got to be kidding me!"

Steve the badger said nothing, but one thing I knew for sure, no way would Nigel have employed a

Wild One if he'd thought he'd get a badger. You'd expect a dog or a tiger or something, but truth be told they were about as rare as, well, a shifter.

I soon changed my mind about Steve's birth curse as the pot-bellied badger, fur bristling, teeth bared, claws scraping against the flour-covered courtyard, dashed forward in a blur of black and white and the gunman went down. Steve snapped tight at his upper thigh and claws raked halfway up the spook's torso.

Jumping out to help, I ran toward them but the animal was overcome with bloodlust and it snarled, warning me to stay away from its prey. I held my hands up, backed off, and as the man screamed and his gun whipped around to the badger's head, his finger readied to fire, Steve raked deep into the man's neck, found purchase, then yanked hard, its body pulled forward as flesh gave way. The badger sank its teeth right into the poor guy's face.

With a grunt and a tug, the man's face was ripped clear away. He gurgled and twitched for a second before he was still.

The badger turned and stared at me with unbridled anger, almost like it was defending its offspring. Slowly, it advanced, fur rasping, oversized teeth stained with gore, small gobbets of flesh trailing from its mouth.

"Um, nice badger. Thanks for the help. Can we, er, go now?" I knew I wanted to, but the last thing I was about to do was turn my back on this powerful creature.

The badger growled as I took a step back, but then it halted and I understood the struggle it was going through. This was the drawback, or one of them anyway, to being a shifter. When the change was complete it was no easy thing to come back from it. I knew many shifters lost themselves to the animal inside and never returned. It took control and a strong will to force your human sensibilities back into the animal, to stop it from overwhelming you completely.

Strange sounds emanated from deep inside the creature's extended belly. The battle for supremacy; man vs beast. But Steve wouldn't be tasked with bodyguard duty if he wasn't an accomplished shifter and soon he began to transform. The change back to human was just as bad, if not worse, than the shift to animal. Bones cracked and flesh reconfigured, and although the metamorphosis took but a few seconds there was a world of hurt experienced in that short time.

Down on all fours, Steve said, "A little help here?" so I held out a hand and hauled him to his feet. Tiny hairs still stuck from his body like a patchy coat, but as the shift completed I watched them recede and the open follicles close, leaving him just a man. Albeit a naked and muscular man with a lot of blood staining his beard and neck.

"Let's get out of here, there'll be more of them. We gotta go." As he spoke, Steve pulled an expensive and strong-smelling pack of wipes from a side pocket of the backpack, wiped himself down with deft strokes and even combed his beard. Satisfied, he drew clothes from his backpack and dressed with practiced efficiency.

"Never knew badgers were so vicious," I said.

"You better believe it," he warned, then pushed open the gates to the alley, checked the coast was clear, and said, "Come on, mate, let's go."

I didn't argue, didn't have time to think, so with nothing better in mind I followed Steve the badger out into the alley. Just before we closed the gates I took a deep breath in through my nose. Boy did the back of a bakery smell nice. My stomach rumbled, but I caught a glimpse of the dead spook and, strangely, the hunger pangs vanished.

New Friends

The Wild Ones were, by their very nature, good at goon work, especially for those in the magical community. Anyone who knows you can turn into a wolf, tiger, even an oversized badger, is gonna think twice before they give you any lip.

Problem being, it also made them volatile and unpredictable. The animal inside didn't care about niceties, about causing a scene, so when they changed you had better be sure there was nobody around to see. Over the years, they'd become adept at keeping their nature hidden, could learn control under the tutelage of the more experienced of their kind, and they stuck together.

They mastered their nature or died, looked out for each other, and weren't above using their violent side if the reward was high. There was no doubt Nigel would have paid them well for this job, and that begged the question, why? Why had Nigel felt the need to have backup goons in addition to his own? What was this all about and what the hell was in the bag?

I kept asking myself the same damn questions over and over, and it was getting on my nerves. I hated being in the dark, liked a mystery about as much as I liked poking myself in the face with sharp sticks, and if I could have kicked Nigel then I would have. Maybe poked him with said sticks, too.

We moved carefully down the alley and I focused on the now. Before we'd got halfway, Steve pulled me aside—which was becoming an annoying habit of his—and moments later I heard footsteps approaching. With our backs to a wall, we weren't exactly invisible, just less of a target, and we both peered down the alley at the same time to see a woman in smart casuals approaching. She was slim and curvy in all the right places, moved with a grace and fluidity of motion that marked her as a Wild One even to my often less than insightful eyes.

The woman stopped in front of us and observed us with hands on ample hips, frowning. "You know people will talk if you hang out in back alleys, right?" She had a lightness to her voice made more attractive by the slightly raw sound—definitely a smoker. Husky yet melodious at the same time.

I wondered what she shifted into. Her hips were wide, sweeping down to shapely legs under tailored trousers, and she wore a smart white blouse that showed off her curves delightfully yet still remained demure and understated. She had absolutely nothing to prove and made a point of showing it, which was kind of a contradiction but trust me, she pulled it off with real style. She had long, wavy blond hair and wore no make-up, which I liked immensely. The hair must have been a dye-job because she had the blackest eyes I'd ever seen on a human. Real spooky.

"Hey, Candy," said Steve.

"Hey, Candy," I said, giving her my best smile. "I'm Arthur."

"I know who you are. We were watching you and Nigel."

"Yeah, not well enough."

She scowled at me and anger flared, so she turned her attention to Steve. "What the fuck was that all about? Simple job, you said. Nice little earner. Just watching the posh twat while he did some nonsense with the wizard. You never said anything about guns and him getting his head blown off." Wow, she was intense. Scary.

I focused on a button on her blouse, just to calm myself, but then realized what I was doing and looked up. She caught my gaze and I knew she knew I knew I was acting like a naughty school kid. Damn, why did sexy women still make me feel like a prepubescent wizard in training?

Steve held his hands up in protest. "Hey, how was I supposed to know? I've done lots of work for Nigel over the years. It always goes to plan. I watch out for him when he doesn't want his spooks involved and there's hardly ever trouble. And never like this. Just the odd chancer, not nutters with sniper rifles."

"Yeah, well, this isn't what I signed up for. Anyway, we dealt with it." Candy flicked her golden locks over her shoulders and I caught a hint of flesh between the gaps in her blouse.

"Dealt with it?" I asked.

"Yes, dealt with it. Meaning, the sniper's dead, and there are two others who are also dead that were after you guys. Plus all Nigel's men are dead, killed by whoever these guys are. Were."

"Damn, you're good," said Steve, smiling and clearly trying to win Candy back over. If he'd begun panting and sniffing her crotch it would have made it no more obvious he had a thing for her.

"Dick," muttered Candy.

"So that's it, then?" I asked. "All the bad guys are dead and the very bad guys, too. No spooks, no people after the spooks?"

"They weren't after the spooks, were they? They were after you and Nigel," said Candy, her focus way too intense.

"Look, your guess is as good as mine why this has gone to shit, but one thing I do know is where there are people trying to kill you there will always be more. It's time for me to go. You guys should leave as well. It's not safe here. The place will be crawling with police as this wasn't exactly done on the quiet."

They knew I was right. The streets would be teeming with all manner of people none of us wished to talk to, and besides, it was obvious that whoever had ordered Nigel shot and had been after me all day wasn't about to stop now.

"What's in the bag?" asked Candy, face turning hard.

"I have no idea, and I don't want to know. Nigel was supposed to take it, but there was something up. Something wrong. A lot of bad people want this, and I wish I'd never set eyes on it."

"So, give it to me," she said. Steve went to speak but she stopped him with a raised palm. No prizes for guessing who was in charge here.

"That a request or an order? Because I can tell you this for free, Candy. You are not getting this bag and I'm doing you a favor. I need to think about this, decide what to do, but I will not hand this over to anyone unless I'm sure that's the right thing to do. Understand?" Much as she was trying to bully and intimidate me, I still didn't wish her or Steve dead, and apart from that I wasn't about to let an unknown magical item loose in the world. That way lay disaster, for all concerned.

Candy shifted her hips slightly, but still dominated with her presence. She was powerful, no doubt, and although I knew the Wild Ones had no leader as such, I was sure that at least in these parts she was someone that called the shots if the need arose. Shifters never took kindly to rules and being bossed about, but they did respect the powerful, and those with intelligence. Steve was clearly in for a considerable backlash for getting them involved in something he would have told his buddies was relatively safe.

"Okay, how many people have you lost?" I asked, trying to convince Candy this was a bad idea.

"None, we aren't amateurs."

She blinked twice and I knew she was lying. "But some got hurt, right?"

"A little," she conceded. "The sniper was well hidden and one of ours got rather bashed about before he brought the guy down."

"And you want to take the bag and remain involved in this? Why not just walk away and forget it ever happened?"

"Because they hurt us, and we don't let that happen," she said.

"Come on, Candy, The Hat's right. This is out of our league. Whatever's in the bag is bad news. We don't need this crap." Steve turned to me. "Arthur, you need to get rid of that and quick."

"Tell me about it. But I can't just throw it in the river. I need time to figure this out."

"When you guys have quite finished?" Damn but she was one bossy lady. "Okay, we're done. But we'll see you home safely, Arthur. Our performance this afternoon was lackluster. Nigel's dead and our pride took a dent. Can we make it up to you?"

I didn't trust her one bit. Either she was fishing for a way to get the bag without causing a scene, or she wanted to hang around to gather more information. Either way, it was not best for me. "That's a kind offer, but unnecessary. I'm used to this kinda thing, it's what I do."

"We know. We know all about The Hat." She cocked her head to the side, and I caught a whiff of her perfume as a breeze ruffled her hair. Damn but she smelled fine.

"Then you know this is nothing you can just go sell to the nearest criminal. This is high end stuff, strictly niche, and all it's brought is death. I'll deal with it, but thanks."

For a moment, I wondered if they'd try to kill me right there and then, but I held myself in check, made no move to wave the old wand at them, and waited it out. If they tried to take the bag then they were a lot more stupid than they looked, and I didn't think they were stupid at all. The Wild Ones may have been a breed apart from average humans but they were smarter, and they had a large community of others they could call on in time of need, but with that came increased responsibility.

They'd already put others in danger by becoming involved in this. If the bad guys felt shifters were in the way then the whole community was at risk, and if that happened there would be severe consequences for Candy and Steve and anyone else involved. Risking bringing down the wrath of an unknown adversary who was obviously unconcerned about killing in public was a big commitment, and I felt confident enough that she wouldn't take that chance.

"Okay, you can go," she said, like she was the boss of me. She wasn't, but I just smiled and said, "Thanks." No point causing more trouble than I already had.

I held out my hand to Steve and we shook. "Thanks for the help, I appreciate it."

"And thanks for not making too many crap jokes about my shift," said Steve, locking eyes, meaning what he said.

"If I caused any offense then I apologize. I run my mouth off when I'm stressed, but thank you for your thanks."

"When you two man-bitches have quite finished with the male bonding can we get out of here?" said Candy with zero interest in our manly ritual.

"Nice to meet you, Steve," I said, sure to say it so he knew I meant it.

"You too, Arthur. Be seeing you."

Steve took off after Candy and she waved over her shoulder, not bothering to turn around.

Nice folks, especially by shifter standards.

Right, time to get home. I had a date and I would not miss it, not for anything. Not even when I had people trying to kill me and steal stuff I didn't even want. Some things were more important, and I didn't miss dinner dates unless things were dire. Or more dire than this, anyway.

Okay, I had no idea what else to do, but I really hated skipping my evening ritual.

Home for Dinner

"It's getting dangerous out there," I said as I dumped the blasted bag in the hallway and took off my boots.

"You look like crap," said George, coming out of the kitchen and heading my way with something so perfect I could have kissed her.

"Ah, what the hell..." I tugged my boot, dropped it, dashed to my daughter and scooped her up in my arms. "Give Daddy a hug." I squeezed her tight, never wanting to let go.

"Geddof me! Put me down, you muppet!" She wriggled and shrieked but I held her tight and made "Mmm," noises as I felt myself more restored than any magic could ever provide. This was the true magic in the world, the true life-giver. Closeness, human affection. Hugs.

There is nothing like wrapping your arms around somebody you care about and them doing likewise. Which was exactly what George was now doing, knowing it was useless to resist, that she'd be stuck there for eternity if she didn't give her old dad a cuddle.

The stress of the day vanished and the worry concerning the night to come faded away as we held each other in the hallway, everything quiet apart from the hum of the extractor in the kitchen and my breathing.

"Okay, old man, time to let go of your hostage and go get your nasty habit over with."

"Thank you, oh darling daughter of mine." I took the lung dart, a hand-rolled delight she now made for me so I didn't use excessive amounts of tobacco, she pulled from behind her ear and winked.

"Idiot."

Holding hands, even though she grumbled, we wandered into the kitchen. She let go and watched from the breakfast bar as I slid the doors into their cleverly designed recesses, allowing cooling air to fill the room. I found my Zippo in a pocket after some nervous, downright frightening searching, then lit up the rollie with excited fingers, lungs already burning with anticipation.

Just outside the kitchen, I took my first drag of the day and held it before exhaling deeply. Smoke drifted away across the garden and I relaxed a little.

"So gross," said George, waving away non-existent smoke from the other side of the kitchen. I was outdoors so she was overreacting a little, but it was for the best, made me be good.

I poked my tongue out at her and coughed happily.

When she moved in, I stopped smoking inside, but she kept on and on at me to stop entirely until I got so fed up with the incessant nagging that I blurted out a promise I regretted as soon as I made it but stuck to more often that not.

I said I'd just have one a day, before dinner.

By this time, we'd settled into life together a little, and I made it a point to always be home for dinner if it was humanly possible. Same for breakfast. But dinner was the main event, the main time we had together, and we made another agreement then. I could have one roll-up, but only if I got home in time for dinner. If I skipped one I skipped the other.

She was a smart kid, no doubt.

George came closer to the doors and said, "Well, what happened? I saw the bag. You didn't give it to Nigel?"

"No. Nigel got shot in the head and I got chased and hooked up with some Wild Ones and—"

"Cool, you hung out with Wild Ones? It's so not fair, you get to have all the fun."

I took another drag, staring with disappointment at the half finished smoke. "I'll have you know it wasn't fun. People were trying to kill me, and in case you missed what I said, someone shot Nigel in the head."

"Probably another spook, you can tell he was up to no good."

"Well, in case you've forgotten, I get up to no good, too. He was my broker, and whatever's in the bag has got everyone acting nuts. Now I don't know how to get rid of it."

"You'll think of something, you always do." For one so young, George was an incredible optimist. Maybe it was the difference between the life she used to lead and her life now. I guess whatever I got up to paled in comparison to the horrors she'd endured. It's all about perspective.

"We'll see." I finished my smoke, held the last lungful until it seeped through my pores, then put it out in the ashtray on the small outdoor coffee table. We went back inside and I closed up.

"You want me to cook?" asked George innocently.

"Haha, you're so funny," I said, stomach doing somersaults just thinking about the horrors she'd presented me with over the last two years. One thing my daughter was not, was a chef. She was an accomplished poisoner of unsuspecting or busy and tired fathers, and after a few "meals" I came to the conclusion that however tired or stressed I was there was no way in hell I'd let her cook again.

And besides, I liked it. It also allowed me to gratify my other vice. Okay, vice that was still legal.

"Put one on and I'll make dinner."

"Aw, Dad, do we have to? It's so ancient, so not funny."

"You take that back right this instant!" I said, smiling at the banter we repeated almost every evening as I made my daughter indulge me.

"Whatever," she said, but nonetheless she moved over to the wall-mounted TV I could see from the cooking island and turned it on. With a few presses of buttons she got up the list and, without asking, picked one at random, just the way I liked it.

For the next half hour I chuckled away to Buster Keaton's antics, admired his pork pie hat, and rustled us up something approaching perfection.

George made salad, set the table, and even laughed a few times, Buster having finally worn her down.

In no time at all we were sitting down to a rather impressive repast of leftover risotto balls stuffed with blue cheese, salmon done two ways, green beans, and a salad she'd only slightly mangled.

We chatted over the meal, me filling her in on the day, apologizing for the bunker incident of earlier, and generally getting her up to speed.

George told me about her day, about the practice she'd done in the attic, the hours she'd put in with her teacher who she'd driven to see in the Mini Cooper I'd got her when she passed her test. It was nice. I said nothing about her having gone out, knew I couldn't make her stay at home all the time. But today was no ordinary day and she knew she shouldn't have left but I didn't push it.

I was trying, even if I got it wrong a lot of the time.

A family. Even if it was slightly dysfunctional.

I did my best, yet knew it wasn't enough. But she didn't hate me, which was something, or so I'd been told by other parents.

All too soon the meal was over and the dishes were cleared away. I sneaked another smoke while she made a phone call to arrange her evening with her friends. I tried not to whoop when she said they were coming over, but she knew it was what I wanted, the only way I'd know she was safe, so she'd done it for me. She was a good girl, although I got the feeling she was only too keen to have her buddies over while I was out, as she knew I'd be away for some time.

Guess a conversation about boys was due soon. When did daughters start getting interested in them? When they were about thirty-five, right? And far away from criminal wizards who will flay the flesh off them if they even look at her funny.

We had coffee when she returned and she only told me off a little about the smoke. Who knows how she knew? A bad father radar is my guess. Then it was the end of my time with my daughter.

She went upstairs to get ready, I used the bathroom and had a quick shower, we said our goodbyes, then I was back out the door and off to the city.

My day was just about to begin. Night was approaching, things began to stir, and no way in Buster's name would the day have a pleasing conclusion.

Still, the salmon was nice. The company even better.

A Jog

I thought of numerous people to call, others I'd have to go visit as they wouldn't speak on the phone, but dismissed them all.

The item was a weight around my neck and it was stupid to involve anyone in something I was in the dark about. Plus, it was clearly so valuable I didn't know who I could trust apart from one person and I didn't want her getting into trouble.

Pepper's treachery was still on my mind, making me doubt everything, even my own judgment. If he could do that to me then who could I truly call a friend?

Deciding that this was gonna play out whether I acted or not, knowing how my life usually went, I decided to go for a quick jog instead.

Running around deserted parks just before dark isn't something I did often, and that was the problem. I was over forty and feeling it. Meaning, things that shouldn't be stiff in the morning were, and things that should be... You get the picture. Exercise was something I'd been trying to get into more, partly because I needed it, but mostly because I was vain and it was nice to look good when stripped down. Not that there'd been anyone to witness the results of my efforts for some time, but that's another story. A much more depressing one.

I wasn't too shabby, slim and stringy, but it wouldn't hurt to have a few extra pounds of muscle and to not get winded so badly when I ran away from people or various creatures as part of work, or sometimes play. I'd taken to running, combining sprints up an incline in a park nobody used as it was out of the way. The whole area had been bypassed by the housing developers and left abandoned. The children's play area little but broken concrete and empty frames where swings had once been, a reminder of the direction the city and the country as a whole was taking.

Nobody came outside to breathe the fresh air anymore, and nobody seemed to care that the patchy grass was going to weeds or that the dog owners who sometimes came no longer cleaned up after their animals.

I slipped my arms through the bag and felt the weight adjust down, the item wrapped in at least several layers of very old and stuffy smelling hessian or something else that stank like it had been stripped off a mummy and bits left inside. Heaving it up so it acted like a backpack, I set off at a slow pace from the car after a few stretches.

Having learned from previous self-inflicted aches and pains, I eased into it, finding my breathing a little easier than it was a few weeks ago. Maybe it was the cutting back of tobacco or the fact I did a few sprints several times a week, or maybe it was that I was free, just running. Feeling the wind on my face and the crisp air scouring my lungs.

I did several quick sprints up and down the hill, then slowed to a walk and wandered aimlessly, sauntering from the cool shade of trees to the warmth of the dying day. I saw a bat flit past, smiled at the call of an owl on early sentry duty, heard ducks overhead and watched their sharp arrow heading west.

"That'd be nice," I said to nobody, watching until my neck hurt and they vanished from my still perfect sight.

Shaking my legs out, enjoying the burn and the feeling of strength, I wondered how nuts I looked to anyone spying. A man wearing a pork pie hat, pockets jangling full of various items, strange leather duffel on his back. Certainly not your average evening jogger.

But I'd given up caring what others thought of me long ago. I knew my own mind, took responsibility for my actions, and knew without a shadow of a doubt that I'd been an idiot for taking the duffel and getting involved with this at all.

Pepper was dead, Nigel was dead. Boris and Mike the goon and that dude on the road, all dead.

There'd be more, no question.

I just hoped one of them wouldn't be me. I might be out of lives, and even if not, it's pretty easy to kill someone again if you've done it once, and then it really would be over. If a keen assailant kept stabbing or shooting me, it wouldn't matter if I had twenty lives, the end result would still be the same.

Arthur "The Hat" Salzman would still be a dead wizard.

A Visitor

"I need to start using weights," I moaned to the pigeon pecking at invisible crumbs by my feet. "Waddya think?" I flexed a bicep but my shirt hid what muscle I had. The pigeon lifted its head and stared at me with rheumy eyes, then hopped away on a malformed leg and continued its spirited pecking—guess it was an optimist and had no time for those on a downer like me.

For the first time since things had taken a turn for the seriously wonky, my thoughts were clear and I could think in a calm manner. It's one thing being chased and given the runaround, blasting and killing those after you, but I'd learned over the years that it's always nice if you have a clue why they are after you.

I leaned back on the old bench, paint peeling and a few of the slats missing, but I didn't even feel the discomfort. My aching body and ragged breathing meant I could have been lying on a camel and I'd still be grateful—I know it looks like fun, trust me, it isn't. Too many humps, and they bite, too.

All I could picture was Nigel's head exploding and then all hell breaking loose. I conjured up the memory of those last few seconds. The way Nigel had acted, the way he seemed to have suddenly come to a decision. It was as if he'd stepped over a line but at the very last moment had decided he wanted to retreat back over onto if not the side of good, then at least not the side of utter evil.

Basically, I had no idea what in Buster's name was going on.

And what had Steve said? That they were paid to protect Nigel, to ensure he collected the item from me and got it delivered. Who, and where, he wasn't so sure, but that was the job.

So, someone had double-crossed Nigel, but had Nigel also cheated his client, or planned to? Surely not? So why the double security? Why not rely on the people he usually had? Why the extra bodies?

Bottom line, it made no sense whatsoever.

"Ugh, what a mess. What am I supposed to do now?" The pigeon wandered off. Looked like I was on my own.

I tensed and reached a hand slowly for my pocket as someone approached. Someone who was being quiet on purpose. A sneak. A thief. A murderer. What was wrong with me? Lost to my own thoughts when everyone was getting their heads blown off or generally getting dead. I could have been shot waiting there like a sitting duck.

Guess it had been a long day already, so I had an excuse. Still, it was stupid.

I released the Velcro, wincing at the noise it made. I should have thought of a better system, maybe a wand holster, but that would just be daft. Or maybe it would be cool? Whatever, too late now.

"My dear boy, no need for that."

I turned in shock at the voice. Maybe I was dreaming, or dead and just hadn't realized. Acting surprisingly calm, I looked into the eyes of the man standing before me and said, "Nigel. You're not dead?"

"Oh, I'm very much dead, dear boy, at least Nigel is. I'm Nathan, his brother. Bit of a shock, I'm sure. May I sit?" I nodded dumbly, my brain taking a while to catch up with proceedings. Yep, definitely in some kind of coma or something. "It's jolly cold out here, even with my scarf," said Nathan, conversationally, like we were two pals just come to feed the local pigeons.

He continued to stand, studying me with a slight frown. I stared right back at him, mind frozen. No thoughts would come, no sudden insights into what was happening or what I should do. Basically acting dumb.

"The wards, if you don't mind?" said Nathan, looking a little perplexed and confused by my actions.

"Oh, sorry, sorry. It's been a long, er, few days."

"I can imagine. The wards?" he hinted again.

"Sorry." I focused best I could and drew them down long enough for him to step inside, then snapped them back into place as fast as I could. I hadn't even realized I'd put them up, but it gave me hope to know that even if I was acting a little—a lot—bewildered there was a part of me still on high alert.

"I apologize for the interruption, but needs must and all that."

"Yeah, right."

"So, here we are," said Nathan.

"Yes, here we are." I turned my focus on him, really looking, and hell did he look like Nigel. There were slight differences, but you'd only know if you really searched for them. I guess the main thing was his facial hair was different. Thick mustache and a clean, weak chin. And the cane and the limp, of course. He rested slim, almost feminine hands on top of the short cane. I may have been in shock but I wasn't too far gone to know it was no normal walking aid. Dude had a serious staff, any wizard could see that. So, definitely not Nigel, even if they looked identical from more than a foot away.

"I can only assume you have had a somewhat stressful day?"

"You could say that."

"I'm taking a big risk being here, and I'm still not convinced I shouldn't just have you killed and wash my hands of this whole sorry mess. You are, Mr. Salzman, a rather slippery fellow."

"Look, buddy, I'm about ready to snap and to be honest I've had it up to here with all this intrigue." I put my hand above my head just to demonstrate how high I was talking about, but Nathan just smiled weakly as if waiting for a child to finish its tantrum.

"I can only imagine."

"Why was Nigel killed? You had something to do with it, right?" I didn't know why, I sure as shit didn't know how a brother could do that to his own, but something told me this Nathan guy had most definitely had his brother eliminated.

"I'm afraid you're correct. Things have got out of hand and taken a turn none of us expected. It's all been a bit of a rush job I'm afraid, and when there's no time for tactics it usually ends up messy. As is the case now."

"As is most abso-fucking-lutely the case. Your brother's head exploded right in front of me."

"A shame. A real shame. Mr. Salzman, will you indulge me? Allow me to explain?"

"Sure, knock yourself out. The bag, right? It's all about the bag."

Nathan glanced at the bag to my right, my hand now wrapped tight around the handle. It was emitting a low glow of anger, almost as if it understood who Nathan was and was less than impressed with whatever he had in mind.

"My brother turned traitor not only on his Queen and country, but on us, Cerberus."

I'd heard the name countless times, who hadn't? A bunch of do-gooders who thought they had the right to decide who could own what. An unsanctioned, pompous, sanctimonious arm of the magical underworld the wizards and magical users and abusers would have nothing to do with. As if it was down to Cerberus there'd be no cool shit lining the shelves in their libraries or any frightening magical items they could show off to their wizard buddies.

"If this is a recruitment drive then I'm not interested. I know all about you bunch of wackos. Go peddle your scaremongering to someone who believes or someone who cares. I just want to get paid and be done with this. I mean, c'mon. You name your 'society' after a three-headed dog that guards the gates of hell so the dead can't leave and think you're onto a winner just because you have a cool name. Doesn't wash with me, buddy, or anyone else. Wizards don't like you guys, you steal our stuff."

"Why, Mr. Salzman, didn't you know? You've been working for Cerberus ever since you first met Nigel."

Just when I thought my day couldn't possibly hold any more surprises.

Revelations

Cerberus was a name everyone in the community knew about, both the darker and lighter side of the underground. The name was Greek, and translates as the Hound of Hades, so its members, rather imaginatively, called themselves Hounds. My guess is because they thought it scared people. I mean, Hound, pretty cool name, I have to admit. The wizard hierarchy —don't even get me started on those guys—hated them because the Hounds make it their duty to stop wizards getting important artifacts, and the criminals hated Cerberus because it meant they, too, found it harder to get what they wanted. The lucrative trade in magical objects and assorted paraphernalia was compromised, which affected the bottom line.

To discover Nigel was working for them came as a shock since I'd believed he was involved in covert government work of one sort or another and had a successful brokering business going on the side. Meaning, he'd get what you wanted if he thought it possible and you paid enough. If this was true, it meant that all these things I'd been getting for Nigel over the years were now in the hands of the Hounds rather than with the honest criminals or powerful wizards I'd assumed had possession.

"Okay, let's start at the beginning," I said knowing I'd get nowhere unless I put all this into some kind of order. Part of me wanted to leave right now, not hear another word, but I knew these secretive types and they weren't the kind of people to let things lie. "First, you were brothers? Twins?"

"Of course twins. We look alike, do we not?"

"You sure do. Okay, so you both work, worked, whatever, for Cerberus?"

"Yes, it has been our honor and our duty for many years."

"Okay, got it. So, why in Buster's name did Nigel get his head blown off earlier?"

"Because of that," said Nathan, nodding at the bag I had absentmindedly drawn close to my leg, knuckles white with the strength of my grip.

"You want it? It's not to be sold? Nigel made me believe somebody was going to be very happy to get this. And I was to be paid," I added.

"That was a lie, I'm afraid. We pay you, Arthur. Can I call you Arthur?"

"Sure, be my guest."

"So, Arthur, this item, it was to be ours, to be locked away and kept from those who would use it to do harm. You must understand, this is a very important item, and it is not to be given to anyone but us. Do I make myself clear?"

Nathan had a hardness to him, a coldness the same as his brother. He was ruthless, I could see that behind his tight smile and his ramrod posture. He was a real player, cold-blooded, single-minded, and would do whatever it took to get what he wanted. What he believed was right no matter what anyone else thought. A zealot, and they're the worst kind of criminal. Why couldn't everyone just be straight up dishonest? It would make life easier.

"So, about the whole Nigel getting shot in the head thing?"

"We found something out this morning and put rather hurried plans in motion to ensure that what we discovered would never happen. It cannot happen. It absolutely cannot."

"Just get on with it. Enough with the crypto-bullshit, okay?" Damn, what was with these guys? Everything had to be so bloody dramatic.

"Nigel was going to deliver the item to those that had requested it from him, believing him to be merely a broker of the esoteric."

I chewed on that for a while, then thought I understood. "So, Nigel was a broker, like everyone believed. But if it was for something important he'd what, keep it for you guys, say he couldn't recover it?"

"Something like that, yes. There are certain items we feel must be kept with us. What better way to get the intelligence we need than from the underground criminal fraternity?"

"Okay, I've got all that. So, Nigel was a Hound? Got stuff for you guys, paid people like me to get said stuff, but changed his mind for this one and decided to actually sell it to those who requested it?"

"Why, my dear fellow, you have it exactly right. All that remains is for you to hand over the item and we are done, our business complete." Nathan smiled in a way that gave me the creeps. It was like a crocodile smiling before it snapped its jaws shut on your head and pulled you under. Cold, emotionless, utterly ruthless. Nathan was an A1 predator of the semi-magical variety and he wasn't asking, he was telling.

"Wait just a minute. So, just to be absolutely sure I know where I stand in all this and understand why my day's been so screwed. You got Nathan shot in the head because I was about to give him the item and he was going to sell it to the person or persons who requested said mystery item?"

"Yes. We've been playing catch-up all day, have had to act in a rather messy, dare I say it slightly unprofessional manner. But needs must and all that. This is important." Nathan turned to me, moving his bad leg with a hand so it crossed over his left. He had nice shoes, and I could tell his socks cost more than most earned in a day.

I let the new information percolate in my mind, snapping into place so I could make sense of things and chew on the crap I was now in, and apparently had been in for some time. No way was I gonna work for these guys, they were as bad as the rest. Worse. They thought they knew best, should control all the miracles in the world. All the rumors, and this new information, made me certain there was a seriously screwed up

123

belief system at the heart of it. Maybe religion, maybe something else, but dudes like this were always zealots and you could never change their mind. Although, Nigel had clearly changed his. I guess money can talk if it screams loud enough.

I jumped to my feet, realization hitting.

"Motherfucker," I whispered, the truth forming in my mind. I was sure of it, it was the most logical, and easiest way to explain how so many people had been trying to ruin my day.

"You've been trying to kill me all day. You sent someone to my home. He threatened my daughter. You set Boris on me. All the other creeps coming out the woodwork, that's all your doing. You turned Pepper against me." The scale of their operation must be huge for them to put things into place so quickly. I'd assumed it was the underground gossip grapevine, individuals acting fast of their own accord, but no, it was the Hounds organizing hurriedly, and when it had failed they'd caught up with us at the cafe and decided to go all out to get what they wanted, no matter the cost to their own or civilians alike. Or me.

Goddamn!

I wasn't getting out of this alive if Nathan would shoot his own brother in the head to get what he wanted.

Decisions

Anger boiled over. "You played me. You and all your ridiculous games. You and your brother. Don't cross me, Nathan, if that is your name. I don't know if your tale about Cerberus is true or not, and at this point I don't care, but I'm not on your side, I'm not on anyone's side. Do you hear me? If I see you again I'll wipe you out. I mean it."

Okay, a little rant, but I felt better. And besides, he'd been trying to kill me.

"Don't take it so personally, Arthur. You must understand, this is an important item and it absolutely must not fall into the wrong hands."

"Oh, and I suppose your hands are the right ones, are they? Who made you judge and jury? You people make me sick. Sanctimonious pieces of shit, all of you. You don't even seem concerned that your brother's dead. But then, if you killed him I guess you wouldn't be too bothered."

Nathan pushed with his cane and got up, almost looking angry. But it faded and he was as cool as Nigel had always been. There was definitely something up with these guys—way too unemotional. Maybe that's what made them so good at what they did. This was beyond government conspiracies but I didn't doubt for a moment Nathan was involved in spy stuff for the government as well. What better cover for pulling all this shit? Same as Nigel. His people were spooks, they had it written all over their faces.

"I won't apologize for trying to stop you giving this to Nigel. I had to act fast and use the contacts available. Yes, we wanted you dead so we could recover the item, and to be honest we had no way of knowing if you had looked, if you knew what it was. We didn't know if Nigel had told you what you were acquiring for him. Did you? Did you look? Do you know what it is?"

No way was I going to give this guy any information. The less he knew the better. "What if I have?"

"Then that would be bad. Very bad. For you and all who you may have told. We can't take that risk."

I knew exactly what he meant by that and it proved me right. The Hounds were nothing but scum. Murderers who would stop at nothing to get what they wanted. "You dare threaten me and my daughter? I've already dealt with one guy today, sent by you, I might add, who made a similar threat."

"Not a threat. Just need to be sure there are no loose ends to tie up. I don't think you know what you have and I don't believe you told anyone, so you may live. If," he warned, lifting a finger and pointing it at me, invading my personal space, "you hand it over. Right now."

His final words echoed in my mind with power. He was using Voice and before I knew it my wards around us dropped and those safeguarding the bag from anyone's hands but my own were also fading. I caught myself, drew the power back tight and wrapped it around me like a blanket on a chilly night.

"Go fuck yourself, Nathan."

I stepped away, keeping my eyes firmly on him.

Nathan shifted forward with a wince, favoring his good leg, leaning on his cane. He studied me for a moment, as if considering what to do with me, like I had no say in the matter, then said, "Very well. I didn't want it to come to this, but you leave me no choice. I will not risk this going any further, it's too important. You will give it to me right this minute or I will be the last person you ever see in this life. I will bring death to you and yours. Obliterate your life."

"Screw you," I said, which I thought summed up the whole mess perfectly.

Nathan turned to the side, nodded at the trees, and then he flung himself aside as the bench erupted into kindling and a thousand stakes and bullets tried to hurt me. Hurt me real bad.

He was surprisingly nimble for a guy with a dodgy leg.

I wasn't quite as fast.

A Welcome Appearance

The bench was little but a pile of matchsticks in less than a second after the barrage of gunfire raked my body and blasted lumps of sod and gravel in all directions.

I held the bullets at bay with my wand in one hand and the bag still clutched tight in the other, the wards that surrounded me in a nifty spirit-shield holding strong enough, for now. But the assault was weakening the protection and me along with it. Hardly brimming with the good stuff to begin with, this was draining me faster than a wizard can sit after being offered a free haircut, and as Nathan clambered to his feet well away from the now erratic gunfire I could tell he knew how I was faring.

"This isn't over. I'll kill every last one of you fuckers for threatening my family."

"Needs must, Arthur. Just hand it over and this will be the end of it. I give you my word as a gentleman."

"Gentleman!" I shouted above the staccato bursts of machine gun fire. "Do me a favor. You just told me you're more than happy to kill little girls, you think I'll let that lie?"

"Some things are way more important than any individual lives, and this is one of those things," he said, shrugging.

You know what? I hated it with an unholy fury when people shrugged their shoulders. It drove me nuts. It's so disrespectful, so downright rude. Nathan may have been many things but he was no gentleman.

The gunfire stopped and I smiled. Nathan turned his head in the direction of the large trees that had given his backup shelter while they tried to kill me, and I took the opportunity to get up close to him.

"Here, you want it then fucking take it."

Distracted by the lack of his goon, and thinking maybe I'd caved because of the pressure—he didn't know me very well if he thought that—he reached out and grabbed the handle of the bag without giving his actions due consideration.

"Sweet dreams, Nathan," I spat, as the wards sprang to life, the magic wrapped tight around the bag doing its job, curled up in a tight ball just waiting to pounce. Sometimes I think these spells, wards, thoughts imbued with the matter of the universe, were almost sentient. They acted so eager to carry out their mission, and once spent they curled back up tight, hibernating like a ferocious animal waiting for the next unsuspecting victim.

Nathan's fingers gripped the handle and I never once let go as the wards coalesced around what they knew was an intruder. A thief. I know, talk about poetic justice, right?

Except this was no quiet, internal process, this was rather sparkly and very, very screamy.

Nathan's mouth stretched taut and for a second his scream was silent, the pain and utter destruction caused by my protective wards so deep and strong and fast it took his vocal chords and brain a moment to catch up with what his body was already experiencing.

His tweed jacket was incinerated up to the shoulder and his shirt along with it. I watched as an expensive Rolex melted off his wrist along with his skin. It was engulfed in an otherworldly flame of darkest umber unlike anything you've ever seen. It brightened once it took hold, burning fiery orange like an angry sun setting as a stormy sky gathered momentum above. Deep, rich, utterly destructive.

His skin seared off, black and crispy flesh revealed beneath the spectral fire. Then his nails blackened and dropped and the remaining skin popped and hissed, tendons twanged and muscles frayed under the extreme magical heat.

Nathan continued screaming even as he raised his cane in his good hand, face a rictus of horror. But there was also a determination there, a focus beneath the wails and the magic that attacked him, creeping up his arm trying to consume him whole for his transgression.

He muttered something unintelligible and his short cane burst into a white light at the tip, a whole helluva lot of sigils springing to life along its length. Cold and uncaring but full of magic, of his will, his spirit. He swiped it once along the arm and with a crunch of bone breaking his fingers snapped open, his hold on the handle released.

It dropped a little but I maintained my grip and stepped away from the horror show.

I knew he was a magic user, but guess it wasn't his main thing. Dudes with guns and thinly veiled threats of spooks and conspiracies was definitely more up his alley.

With his grip released, the wards snapped back into their tight circle of protection and I took another few steps away.

"Oh, well, don't say I didn't offer."

"You'll pay for this. Nobody disobeys Cerberus. You don't know what you're doing, what you have," he hissed.

"No, but I do," said somebody behind me.

I knew it wouldn't be a friend.

Um, Oops!

"I don't suppose you'll hand this over nicely and we can all go about the rest of our day?" asked the man who very calmly, and with a confidence I knew in my bones wasn't for show, came into sight and stood between Nathan and I. He was unremarkable, bland in every way. Dressed smartly in a suit you'd be hard pushed to recall, and his features were the same. Just a bloke you saw every day, nothing special about him apart from the fact he was so unremarkable you couldn't describe him however hard you tried.

I ignored the question and asked one of my own. "Guess you're who stopped the goon shooting at me?" I wondered if it was a good time to run or not.

"No, it isn't," said the man.

This was bad, and I may go so far as to say it was utterly, totally, incredibly not good, and I'm not just being dramatic. He could hear my thoughts.

Nathan was soaked in a sickly sweat, close to passing out, but somehow, and I couldn't help admiring his fortitude whilst at the same time hating his guts, he managed to remain upright and focused. But shock was a bitch and it wouldn't be long before he was unconscious, and dead, unless someone happened to call for an ambulance. I was about as inclined to do that as the dude standing between us.

"You... can't... have it," croaked Nathan, the words coming out almost garbled between gritted teeth. He began to drool, a long string of saliva that hung from the corner of his mouth like he was a dog tied up just out of reach of a meaty bone.

"Oh, Nathan, must we really do this again? So many times you have tried to take the things we want, and even succeeded on occasion, but I believe this time you're well and truly beaten. The wizard has defeated you, and I understand he had an agreement with your deceased brother. Very cold and cruel of you, to go to such lengths. You have my congratulations for trying so hard."

Okay, this was getting creepy now. How was Nathan still standing? Magic, that was why, but not enough to save him. And who was this guy and what history was there between them?

"Please, one moment," said the man, and he stepped over to Nathan and kicked the cane out from under him.

Nathan fell and the man stared down at him then bent and picked up the cane. He turned to me, inspected the faint markings, and said, "Another item that belongs to us and was taken by these fools." He tilted it expertly between his fingers, then, keeping his eyes on me, he slammed it down hard onto Nathan's ruined arm.

Nathan screamed and the pigeons that had just alighted after the trouble took to the air once more. If they knew what was good for them they wouldn't be back any time soon. The shock of it must have been too much for poor old Nathan and his eyes turned up in his head. He was out cold, soon to be dead.

"Us?" I said. "Who's us?" It always helps to get confirmation under such circumstances.

"Haha, The Hat playing games with me. What a delightful day this has been so far, and it will only get better."

"Is that so?" I asked, knowing mine would go the opposite way.

"Yes, and we have your payment waiting for you back at the residence."

"Let me guess, and you've come to take me there?"

"Unless you have any objections?" he asked, head titled to one side as if the idea was quite unheard of.

"I get the feeling I have little choice in the matter. By the way," I said, "who are you?"

"Oh, I'm just a, what do you like to call it? A goon? Haha, I'm just a goon."

"If you say so, buddy. I meant your name. What's your name?" This was definitely no goon, but he seemed to think I knew who he was, or who he worked for, so I didn't let him think otherwise.

"You don't need my name, we won't become friends," he said. "I'm here to ensure the deal struck with Nigel is fulfilled, and to see to it you are brought to the others so we get what we asked for and you get what you requested as payment."

"Lead the way, oh man of mystery," I said, giving Nathan a kick as I headed in the direction the mystery man pointed to with his newly retrieved cane.

I heard another grunt behind me and turned to see the man bending and waving the staff over Nathan. Then he dropped it and stood, seemingly satisfied.

"You not going to kill him?" I asked, surprised.

"Do you think us monsters? I am ensuring he doesn't die from his wounds. You hurt him badly."

"That was the intention. And, um, yeah, I do. Maybe. It's complicated."

He frowned in puzzlement for a moment then smiled. "Ah, a joke. They said The Hat was funny. Monsters, haha." Then the smile faded and he was no longer by Nathan's side but inches from my face, staring at me hard and without an inkling of emotion.

He revealed a little of himself, just a taste. He was a monster, and apparently I'd struck a deal with him and his buddies.

I'd met only a few like him in my life, for his kind didn't often mix with mine, but after staring into his eyes I knew exactly who, or what, I was dealing with.

Vampires.

I know. Double "Eek!" right?

All of a sudden everything Nathan said made a little more sense. Not a lot, but a little. Nathan and his fellow Hounds had believed the death of children and their own family was worth it to stop the vampires getting the item.

With magic almost gone, and no way for me to deal with this guy and survive, mainly because there were another five that looked just like him already waiting by the trees, I gripped the bag and walked up to the limousine waiting for me with the door already open.

The sun set behind the trees and the birds sang their farewell as dusk settled over the land and dark thoughts and darker deeds filled my mind.

At least I was exiting in style.

A Ride

There was one thing to be said for the elusive and secretive vampire community, they had style. Class. They surrounded themselves with the good things in life, had taste mostly born from their long lives and their inheritance from their maker, and were usually very polite. Right up until they tore out your throat or drained your essence in any number of exciting but deadly ways.

The Five that accompanied me—for I was sure he was a Five—was a case in point. He was respectful, charming, helpful, and polite. And downright scary because of it.

The driver was probably just a regular driver, one of the fanboys. A human who knew of their existence and had somehow—and it ain't easy—managed to not only find them, but to get into their inner circle and do what it took to gain their trust and the promise of future immortality.

I could count on one hand the number of vampires, or sub-vamps, I had met in my forty-three years on the planet, and this was the longest conversation I'd ever had with one.

All other encounters had been more of a, "Well, you're gonna eat me so I'm gonna blast you until you're in little bitty pieces and can't come after me again," variety, but mostly they stayed right out of human affairs. Yes, they didn't see themselves as humans, much like a chimp wouldn't see itself as an orangutan if you asked it and it could answer without just nicking the bananas and doing a runner up the nearest tree.

After getting in the car, we chatted about nonsense while we drove through the city, making it all the more surreal. My escort was quite a chirpy fellow for a vampire, and much better company than any others I'd met, mainly because he wasn't trying to eat me, but the real reason why it was all so genial was because I had the bag and they wanted it more than anything else.

I was safe. For now.

The conversation dried up and I sank back into the luxurious leather, trying to come to terms with the way my life had changed in the space of a day.

I began to get nervous. Very nervous. Why did everyone want it so badly? Cerberus were willing to off a rather infamous wizard—me, The Hat—to ensure it didn't go to the vampires, and that took real balls. Not only would they have been well aware of who I was and that I was a face, known by those in our world, but they would also have known they'd risked exposure by sticking their necks above the parapet and letting the vampires know Hounds were involved and wanted the item.

Same for the vamps. They were incredibly secretive, never came into contact with wizards, and certainly not Hounds. Everything was topsy-turvy and it all meant one thing. Bad news for Arthur.

Everyone was acting irrationally.

You never met anyone who would admit to being a Hound. It went against what every practicing wizard or magical adept I'd ever met believed in. Heck, we all got where we were with a little help from a magical object or two, me being no exception. Hint, it's on my head and keeping my scalp warm.

We loved us a weird, mystical object, and that's why I ended up doing what I did. It was one step from buying and selling to stealing from those that either didn't know what they had, or really shouldn't as it could blow up in their face. A magical merry-go-round where items were forever changing hands, usually because of me or someone like me, but obviously not as good.

Now everyone had gone crazy. Showing themselves, killing in crowded places, walking around with canes most criminals would sell their grannies to own, and even the vampires were out in the day—or dusk, anyway—albeit only for a short while. The Fifth beside me had struggled to make it to the car, but he remained strong even though his body and will were clearly weak. If he'd been out in daylight for much longer, I was sure it would have been the end of him.

And me, lucky me, I was apparently being taken to see a man I could only assume would be a Second. A Third at least.

Joy!

An hour or so later, with darkness now almost complete, the car slowed and a large double gate opened. We wound our way up a sweeping drive to a house located on the top of a rise, the landscape going on for miles in every direction. If you wanted a home that could be easily defended because you could see anyone approach then you didn't get better than this.

The house was bloody huge.

The extent of the vampire community in the UK was pretty much non-existent, same as it was worldwide. The Family as a whole was large, an immense infrastructure, much like a corporation, that had its hand in every aspect of business of an illegal variety, but they never dealt with it personally. They had people.

As to actual vampires, it was anyone's guess. But we assumed their numbers were minimal and each year they became more secretive and withdrew further from the concerns of humans.

Hell, nobody even knew who ran things, how many true vampires there were, or where they were based. At least nobody I'd ever met. They took privacy to a whole other level of paranoia, and it's easy to understand why. People would try to kill them and who needed the hassle?

If the word on the street was right then you were looking at maybe a few hundred real vampires worldwide, the subs maybe numbered in the thousands but were nowhere near the level of a Second.

And I was about to go say hi.

The Handover

"Yours, I assume," I said as I stood before a man who was so forgettable I had to focus for him to even really register. I think that without my magic I would have walked right past him, forgetting him the moment I saw him. Like he was a piece of plain furniture or a pot plant.

"Hopefully," he said, looking to my right where the Fifth stood close, threatening in a nonthreatening way. You had to be there. Trust me, he was ready for action.

"Oh, sorry. Haha, forgot." I let the wards go from the bag and the symbols floated up and danced around in a flourish like musical notes then winked out of existence.

"Very impressive," said the Second, for it was him, I was sure.

"It's all about the drama," I said, knowing if I hadn't released the wards things would have gotten nasty and I'd be having another chat with Death—a very long one.

"Problems?" asked the Second of the Fifth.

"The Hat is what some would call a lucky man. Fortuitous. Nigel is dead, Nathan has an injury but will recover."

"How unfortunate. I hope you remained professional, showed mercy even of our enemies?"

"I did."

These guys really took their roles seriously. Vampires played it straight and didn't do anything that could get them into trouble with the law or other more deadly forces unless absolutely necessary. It was a survival thing, too few to risk losing even one of their members. Sure, they were criminals, but good ones, and there's a big difference between the working man and the one that runs the show.

"If you please?" asked the Second, holding out a hand.

I took in the lavish yet understated and very stylish room I'd been led into, a library of sorts, rammed with all manner of objects and books I would have loved to have a few weeks to go over, and the line of expectant men, women, and vampires standing a respectful distance behind the Second, and knew I had no choice.

So, I handed the bag to a very nondescript, plainly dressed, utterly forgettable man. He wore a simple black suit of very high quality with a timeless cut and zero ostentation. Had an average haircut on an average face and when he spoke his voice was entirely indistinctive.

The kind of person you'd forget in a heartbeat. You could never describe him as there was nothing to describe. You couldn't pick out where he bought his clothes or shoes, or remember his scent because he didn't have one.

His hands were slender but I knew they were strong, incredibly so. Superhuman, some might say.

"Thank you," he said as he took the bag from my outstretched hand before I had chance to change my mind.

And change my mind I did.

Thin, pale, and average lips parted to reveal a set of typically British teeth. Neither sparkling nor ravaged by time, uneven or too even, just average. Apart from the two incisors, which were sharp, very sharp, and twice as long as they should be.

For a moment, just a fleeting moment so brief as to be questionable, he flickered and his true self shone through. Far from forgettable.

"I done a bad thing, right?"

"Depends on your outlook, I suppose."

"It's him, isn't it?"

"It is," the Second conceded.

"Bugger. Shall I take it off your hands? Maybe bury it somewhere deep and cover it with concrete? Throw it into a nuclear reactor or something?"

"They said you had a penchant for jokes, I shall assume that was one."

"Assume what you like, but just don't assume this means we're buddies."

"Haha, whatever makes you think I want to be your friend?"

"Oh, you know, the winning smile, the jovial manner. The hat. Everyone loves my hat."

The Second handed the bag to a goon he beckoned with the crook of a finger and then he stepped forward, way closer than I'm comfortable with vampires getting.

"Thank you, Arthur. This has been a trying time for you, I am sure. For all of us. But it is over now, and you may leave."

"Oh," I said, surprised. "Right, okay then. Be, er, seeing you."

I turned, waiting for a stab in the back or a bite to the neck, feeling utterly exposed as I took one slow, unhurried step after another. No point acting scared, now wasn't the time for weakness.

"Oh, Arthur?"

Buster's hat! I knew it was too good to be true. I turned and said, "Yes?"

"Haven't you forgotten something?" he asked, eyes dancing with amusement.

"Don't think so. Did I leave my toothbrush? You keep it, you need the work."

"No, Arthur, your payment for services rendered. For retrieving the item for me. For us."

"I assumed that part of the deal was off now."

"We are creatures of our word, Arthur. Children of the Blood never go back on their word. What are we without our word, our reputation?"

"Nothing, we're nothing."

"Exactly."

With the slightest wiggle of a finger, another goon stepped forward and it was clear this one was vampire too. The Second took the package from him then waved him away with a relaxed hand.

He held out the payment to me and I walked back and put a hand to the slim, beautifully wrapped package. He gripped it tight, took my gaze and held it for the longest time, then said, "May I ask you a question?"

"Sure, as long as it's not about anything too personal."

"Why this? Of all the things you could have asked for, even not knowing what the item was, why this? You could have had money, a lot of money, other things far more valuable. Ancient books, powerful objects, so much. Yet you asked for this specifically. I am curious."

"Sorry, that is too personal a question."

"Ah, the sentiment of humans, it never fails to impress, confuse, and confound me." The Second released the package and I took it, pocketed it, then fastened the Velcro.

"Well, be seeing you."

"You can count on it."

I got the hell out of there before he stopped me again.

Another Job Done

The journey home was interminable. I couldn't believe I'd been so stupid. I also couldn't believe I'd been so damn lucky. Lucky to get out of there alive, lucky to have survived long enough to hand over the item, and lucky enough to have been paid in full.

The item?

Yeah, about that. I realized the moment I stood before the Second. I saw it in his eyes no matter how well he tried to hide it. The hunger in the faces of the others, the tense atmosphere and countless other signs made me sure I was right about what I'd delivered.

This was why Nathan killed his brother, why they tried to kill me and take the bag. Why Cerberus had exposed themselves, killed openly and done anything they could to get it the moment they knew about it being in my hands.

Everything made sense and I saw the Hounds in a whole different light. Yes, they were up their own asses, but this time, for this, they were maybe right even if they'd gone about it in a rather extreme way.

I guess they'd believed they couldn't trust me, but if they'd told me what it was and asked nicely, not even paid me, I would have gladly handed the damn thing over. I wouldn't have touched it no matter the price if I'd known what it was.

Curse Nigel. He deserved to die for what he'd got me involved in. What he'd got everyone involved in.

The bag contained the ashes of Mikalus. The first vampire. Known, like you couldn't guess, as the First. He was like the Holy Grail for the vampires.

He was legend. A story, a fable, a myth, or many thought of him as such. I'd only ever half believed the stories of him when alive, or dead but alive if you know what I mean, but there had always been whispers about the first true vampire, about his remains, his ashes.

Centuries ago, maybe close to a thousand years, he was born, and he lived for many hundreds of years, spreading the virus he became infected with through misuse, or probably downright abuse, of magic.

There are terrible creatures lurking in the Nolands, and he'd called up something he should never have called forth. An illegal and very stupid summoning of something that should have been left well alone. He was attacked and bitten—although the stories often differ—slowly changing into the vampire to beat all vampires. The original and the best, all those that came after, especially later generations, little but poor imitations. The true power and strength he was endowed with never quite transferring over to those he baptized into his perverted flock.

The story went it took a long time for him to realize his true potential, and only after many years did he understand what it was he had become. Slowly losing the battle with his body and mind, until eventually he died and was reborn as a being at one with the creature he'd unleashed and battled before somehow sending it back to a corner of the Nolands it called home.

He was reborn as vampire, immortal and powerful, and his domination grew until it encompassed much of Eastern Europe and had spread around the globe, a select few, a very select few, brought into the fold and given his gifts.

But he got sloppy, a single careless act and his life was forfeit. Back then life was harder and simpler, and somehow, by some silly error, maybe a fallen curtain or a tear in fabric, maybe a dislodged stone or a careless footstep, or, and some believe this to be the case, a purposeful ending of his own life, the sunlight hit his flesh and he was turned to ash. Instantly combusted, the daylight anathema to true vampires because of where this disease originated, from a creature that never knew daylight, didn't even really understand the sun and the ways of our world. A creature born of the darkness.

Whether he took his own life or whether it was taken from him, the legend went that a faithful servant, a human—for very few earned the right to be turned—gathered up his ashes in a simple wooden box and after that the mystery deepened.

Every decade or so, there was a new rumor about Mikalus' box. Stirrings and whispers in the preternatural world as the underground went into a frenzy of searching, offering ridiculous bounties, and the chase was on in one corner of the globe or other. Nobody ever found it.

Until me.

The most ridiculous part?

Obtaining it was one of the easiest jobs I'd ever undertaken. Simple, quick, and painless.

It just went downhill after that. I don't think anybody but the vampires and maybe Nigel, Nathan, a couple others, knew what I was carrying, and they certainly weren't talking. If those in our world knew what I had, you can bet they would have moved heaven and earth to get their hands on it. Many would do anything, including drop a bomb on the city, to ensure the box never got into the wrong hands. I didn't blame them. Others would have been just as keen to get it and try to reanimate him and make him do their bidding.

I knew better.

Mikalus was the original, the true source of pure vampire blood, everything else a weak, pathetic approximation of what it was like to be truly vampire.

Sure, the old ones were ultra strong, but the newer vamps were just softies. Kids in comparison.

Now they had him. I'd given Mikalus' ashes to them.

I'd unleashed hell on earth.

Almost home, the darkness of the countryside enveloping me in silence and a strange, hollow feeling inside, I slammed on the brakes and shouted, "Ah, fuck it!" and banged my hands on the steering wheel before going off on a mad tirade of ultra-extreme cursing and general despairing at what I'd got myself into.

I couldn't leave them to it, much as I wanted to just go home and forget the whole sorry incident. No, I had to do something.

The Hounds would be after me. I'd be enemy number one for handing it over no matter what I told them, and Nathan was probably a little annoyed about his arm. By Buster's hat, the vampires would be unstoppable with Mikalus restored to his previous good, everlasting health—as long as he invested in decent curtains and wrapped up properly in the daytime.

Cursing, and carrying on cursing, I turned the car around and headed right back the way I'd come.

Criminal with a conscience, a bad combination.

But I guess I was a little to blame, what with the whole handing over the nastiest, most powerful, immortal ex-human in history to a bunch of vampires and all. So, there was that.

I needed a drink first, though.

No, I needed something much more potent to relax me.

I went to Satan's Breath.

Stinky Wizards

Wizards got sweaty, and when they got sweaty they smelled. Bad. Very bad.

I was no exception. Maybe it was the strain of imbibing the nature of the universe itself—which, let's face it, is pretty miraculous—or maybe it was the extreme focus it took to control said magic, let alone channel it, use it, morph it and bend it to my will. Or maybe the real reason was because we got chased so much and were rather unfit. Either way, we got a little whiffy, so, above all else in the world apart from wielding elemental forces and doing stuff we probably shouldn't, we loved us a sauna.

On the outskirts of the city, surrounded by the detritus of consumerism gone bad, the unfinished warehouses, and small businesses struggling to stay afloat, where scrub had replaced manicured landscaping long ago abandoned, and you felt a million miles away from the hustle and bustle, the cosmopolitan feel, the back alleys teeming with ne'er-do-wells, and the private clubs and meeting places of the underground, sitting alone surrounded by tall, majestic oaks is a building.

Constructed by a man with more money than sense, it was his idea of giving something back to the community of magic users. Something special, something that was ours, something functional.

Wizards weren't big on function, they were big on messing about with things they shouldn't and getting into lots of trouble. So, inevitably, this wizardly wonder had its quirks. I'm convinced the true reason why this magnanimous benefactor built this was because he stank and wanted others to admit the same.

The end result was a strangely out of place building, somehow overlooked by the industry that came and mostly went from the city, standing isolated as it did surrounded by scrub and broken fencing from the days when its neighbors were wealthier.

It was a modest but elegant building, all thick lumps of stone, taking design influences from Turkey and the more ancient Roman bathing houses, but from the outside it looked like little more than a large blocky building with a rather nice portico entrance.

Don't let the name put you off, it was truly one of the best experiences of your life—although, obviously, it's wizards only.

Welcome to Satan's Breath.

It'd had several owners over the centuries, but the current owner was the only one I'd ever known. He was as permanent a fixture as you could get in our world where faces were the same until poof, one day they've just disappeared. It happened a lot, especially to the novices and the older guys. The young ones did something stupid and went up in smoke, the older ones dug too deep and their power became uncontrollable, or they called forth something they shouldn't and found themselves dragged off to some section of the Nolands. Or went there voluntarily if they happened to summon something that could guide them through the nicer parts.

I had no intention of doing either. I wanted to live a long and fruitful life and go out in a way unrelated to magic. Yeah, there was fat chance of that happening, right?

I parked up between vehicles that told the story of the life of wizards. Some were expensive Bentleys and other status-symbol vehicles, others were battered Fords or station wagons, a few trucks, and even several bicycles. Modes of transport running the gamut of the world we lived in. Rich to poor, most of the owners living lives far from respectable and usually making their way through this thing called life on the wrong side of the law the country would have us live by. Ha, if only they knew what we got up to.

We had our own laws and we lived by those. Many magic users hardly gave the rules the general population mostly abide by even slight consideration. Magic, it attracted a certain kind of person, and that person was usually someone looking for something different to the world they'd been told was all that reality contained. They wanted more, to uncover secrets and look behind the veil. Many hated what they saw, others, like me, were the opposite. Some were simply desperate, searching for a way out of poverty or the mundane life they felt trapped in. When they got a taste of the power, it's understandable they saw the way the world functioned in a very different light.

Or maybe it really was just me and I'm looking for a reason to explain why I behaved the way I did and ran in the circles I ran in. Often, it felt like I had no choice, but even then I was old enough and ugly enough to know that was an excuse. And a lame one at best.

I loved this stuff. It was what made me The Hat. But it meant I got stinky so it was time for some relaxation and cleansing.

The Gossip

As I stepped into the cool of the expansive foyer, the space much larger than the entire building from the outside—proper Dr. Who style—I felt like all eyes were upon me. I tried to act casual, but the moment you think about how you are holding yourself, where you look, who you make eye-contact with and what you do with your arms, you become so aware of your body and your every action that you may as well be holding up a sign saying, "Hey, look at me! I done summit bad and you all already know, don't you?"

I caught myself just before I began to hum a tune, a sure sign I had something to hide.

The walk across the intricately tiled floor, each tiny piece taking an imp a year to make, seemed to take an eternity, so I took the time to adjust my hat, smooth out the wrinkles in my shirt, and tap the package in my pocket just so I knew the day hadn't been a dream. Nope, it was real. Bummer!

"You've been a naughty boy," said the Turk, owner and man of mystery. He rubbed at his hairy chest, partially concealed only by a white vest, the brittle black strands in a perpetual state of trying to make a break for freedom in any direction they could.

"Eh, what? You've heard?" From what the Second had said, I'd assumed I was on safe ground here, that less people than I'd at first believed knew what I'd taken. Only Cerberus and the vampires in the know. Surely nobody knew what I'd given them?

"Heard? Heard what?" asked the Turk, large belly jiggling as he bent to a pile of towels and handed me a couple.

Aah, the feel of fresh, soft towels. Nothing like it. I was itching to get into the steam room, but the Turk seemed to have no intention of letting me go just yet.

"Um, nothing. Sorry, bit distracted. What can I do you for?" Guess this was about something else, which was a mighty relief. I put the sweat down to the anticipation of getting steamy, but considering it was always cool in the foyer that didn't really wash. He didn't seem to have noticed.

"You forgot to renew your subscription. It was up last week. The Turk is not happy," said the Turk, scribbling in the large book always open on the small table he seemed to spend half his life behind. The other half spent sweating and pouring cool buckets of water over his powerful, gross, hairy frame. He also liked to talk about himself in the third person, which was kinda fun. Made him sound like a wrestler.

"Oh, ah. Sorry. You know you should just do direct debit, right?"

"Don't trust all that technology," he said, looking at me from under heavy lids like I'd cursed all things wizardly.

"It's how everything works now, Turk, you should get with the times."

"Arthur, the Turk has lived for many hundreds of years, has seen more than you will ever know, and one thing he is certain of is that this computer business is just a passing fad. What happens when the power goes out? Eh? Tell the Turk that. Where will his money be when all the computers get fried or some numpty somewhere puts in the wrong numbers or misspells his name?"

I said nothing, knowing I couldn't win such an argument with the Turk. Just grunted.

"Exactly," he said, smug, then scribbled in his book some more. "Right, the Turk will put you down as a yes for annual subscription renewal, you'll find your bill waiting on your way out. Pay it within the week or you know what'll happen. The Turk has a waiting list, so don't forget."

"I won't. Thanks, Turk."

For months after I started coming, I felt extremely uncomfortable calling the Turk "The Turk," feeling it to be a racial insult. But it was what he referred to himself as, and to be honest I think he did it just to act mysterious, but mainly as a tax dodge and to keep any other wizards from trying to hack him. Even though he was so paranoid he wouldn't let you use your phone inside Satan's Breath—his wards blocked all technology more powerful than a light bulb.

I used to ask him his name, ask what I should call him, and he would freak out, thinking I was a wizard spy out to get him and do despicable things to his business. So Turk it was and Turk it remained.

It was doubtful he was even from Turkey. He had a mild Northern accent, but also sported a big mustache and that seemed to be enough for everyone else to take him at face value. Whatever, he ran a tight ship and what happened in Satan's Breath stayed in Satan's Breath. It was our oasis in the desert, our ship in the most dangerous of seas. Cheap, too.

I took my towels, went into the locker room, and greeted various men in disconcerting states of undress —the only real downside to the place. Naked wizards were not a thing of beauty, more concerned with exercises of the mind than the body, and there were way too many saggy bits and dangly bits for my liking but life's all about sacrifice.

My locker, like all others, had no key, but rather a ward given to me each year that changed. Summoning up the counter ward, I reached out with my mind and positioned one over the other. The door swung open, along with the shield that gave me utter privacy.

Think of it as a safety deposit box for wizards, the place as much a bank as somewhere to get clean. Inside, I had various bits and pieces I wanted to ensure remained safe, plus several changes of clothes for all seasons, heavy on the rainy weather for that's what was most likely.

I stripped down to my hat, wrapped a towel around my waist, locked up, and put my dirty clothes at the end of the row of lockers—they'd be clean when I returned.

First I took a warm shower, soaping and scrubbing until I glowed pink, then turned up the heat in preparation for the inferno to come.

Once as clean as a fish in water, I padded barefoot through one of several arched entrances that led to the main attraction. The steam room.

The pool at the center was super-heated, almost scalding, and dotted around the impressive circular room were large pits with hot stones tended by novices who poured water on them to keep the air just below a temperature that would boil your blood.

Wizards relaxed in various states of lobster-like contentment on recliners, others sitting at the edge of the pool dangling their knobbly, pale legs. Several hardened souls were actually in the water, gasping for breath, skin puce, eyes bleeding.

I activated the wards in my hat and blissful cool air swirled lazily across my scalp, keeping my brain at a cool temperate so I remained sharp and didn't have a seizure. Picking a vacant recliner I leaned back, put my arms behind my head, and sighed. Relaxed for the first time that day.

What was I to do? I knew this was bad, very bad, but the scale of it hadn't quite filtered through yet. I knew I wasn't entirely to blame, people had been trying to kill me all day, after all, and I didn't know what I had until it was too late, but still, I was the one who'd finally got my hands on the First and I'd handed him over like he was little but a stolen piece of jewelery.

I figured I had a little time to come up with a plan, but how much I had no idea. Would they have everything ready for whatever creepy ritual they had to perform to get him reanimated? How did they go about doing it? It wouldn't be straight necromancy as there was no body as such. This would call for something much more serious involving one helluva lot of magic.

Who could do such a thing? Would the Second—or maybe there were a few here?—be strong enough to call him forth? I honestly didn't know. If you think wizards and magic users are kinda private then you ain't seen nothing until you try to find out about vampires and what they're capable of.

After all this time, all these years, they were almost dismissed as being of no importance. Their numbers so low, their influence on others in the life so weak compared to what it had once been, and the truce between wizards and vampires having held for so long, that nobody gave them a second thought.

Until now. Until me.

Where's the Water?

I couldn't relax, couldn't let my mind drift and for a solution to present itself.

I needed information, something to go on. A way to retrieve the ashes of Mikalus before he was dragged away from whatever corner of hell he currently resided in. If not, the world would soon be a very different place.

As I paced, getting dizzy with the heat, a sudden, some would say rare, insight came to me. The reason why I was here. I was afraid. I was afraid to be alone, to deal with this, so I'd sought sanctuary. Safety in numbers. Knowing nobody would try anything here, in a place surrounded by wizards and strictly off-limits for violence within the community.

Other magic users knew exactly what the place was, those simply criminals thought it a weird private club for dodgy looking blokes with beards that needed a good going over with a hedge trimmer and an update to their wardrobe.

I was hiding.

Coward.

The words reverberated around my skull, taunting me, yelling, until I couldn't focus or think of anything at all. I ambled over to the pool and slumped, hardly aware that my feet were submerged over the side.

I was sweating even more than I should have been. My body felt like every drop of moisture had been sucked out of me and I was dessicated, all dried up. Ash, just like vampire number one. I shook to clear my mind, knowing I was just tired from the craziness, and my lethargy and lack of magic was having a very adverse effect on my focus. For with magic came the ability to consider its implications, how it could help you, and more than anything that was the mistress I sought.

Slowly, everything faded away, and I pictured myself in my room at home. Naked, silent, connected to the no-state, the non-being. Emptiness and power, forces so magnificent they defied description, filtering into me, making me whole and enabling this tiny, puny human to become something more than he maybe should. Everything muted down to such a low level that the magic we think of as powerful is little but a pathetic spark of base energy once it's gone through the leveling effects of such a frail body.

I sat like that for maybe an hour or longer, just absorbing the power, everything joining back up inside me like one of those connect-the-dots picture books. I sweated until I felt clean inside and out, and I was resolute. Mikalus had to be destroyed once and for all. I had to stop the vampires before they resurrected him.

I smiled at my own panic, my own fear. This wasn't who I was. I was The Hat and I demanded respect.

The waves of the pool lapped against my legs, washing over my thighs and scalding them, but I didn't mind, was used to it now. They weren't normally this strong, though. Must mean those in the pool were moving about and causing ripples. Then a large wave splashed right up to my chest and I opened my eyes as the shouts and screams began.

Suddenly, like someone had pulled out the plug, the water sucked down through a massive gaping hole in the bottom, heat roared up, fire and steam hissed and a strong smell of sulfur hit, making it hard to breathe.

"Where is the mortal known as Arthur?" asked what I can only describe as a cross between the creature from Alien and a warped demon's idea of a way to terrify naked wizards. It wore a white capirote that towered up to the ceiling, a conical pointed hat with a mask joined, two rough eye-slits glowing red. Massive horns poked out either side of the capirote, the rest of its huge, sculpted frame naked and bristling with tight bunches of powerful muscle.

The water cascaded off its body, steaming as it evaporated. The sub-demon turned slowly in a circle, inspecting the wizards like maggots as they jumped out of the water or were pulled out. Surrounding the pool, a bunch of undressed wizards, me included, waited.

The ancient being focused its gaze on me.

"Damn, Turk," I whispered, "didn't you think to set wards underneath the bloody building as well?"

Guess not, as otherwise old steamy here wouldn't have come visiting.

Which was a shame, because sub-demon or not, he was damn big and damn scary.

A Little Help

The one thing you have to understand about those involved in magic is most of them were none too keen on fighting those more powerful than themselves. Which was entirely understandable. So it came as no surprise to find that the numbers had thinned rather quickly and more than half those in attendance had scarpered.

"You are he," came the booming voice of the unwelcome guest.

"Says who?" I said, wishing I hadn't dropped my towel as it made me feel less wizardly. I also missed my wand. Actually, just being somewhere else entirely would have been ideal.

"It's him, it's him," said a lowlife across the other side of the room.

"You dirty traitor," I shouted, and there were murmurs of agreement. You don't rat. Ever.

"You're banned," shouted the Turk, incensed that someone would tell on another. "Out. Now. The Turk has spoken."

The guy protested but the Turk turned his back to him and he left, head bowed. Served him right. Or maybe it was a sneaky ruse to get out with his life, in which case lucky bugger.

"You're gonna pay for this," said the Turk.

"Don't blame me," I protested. "I didn't invite it here. Why haven't you got wards for this kind of thing?"

"Because it's only the third time it's happened, and underground wards are a bitch," said the Turk.

There were more murmurs of agreement. He had a point, they really were a bitch to do.

"Anyway," I said to the demon, "Arthur isn't here." I know, it was lame, but I had to try.

"I was told the mortal wears a hat. You have a hat."

"Lots of mortals, er, people wear hats," I said, wishing I didn't right now.

The creature took a quick look around the room and said, "No. Just you."

Damn, time for some action.

"A little help here, guys?" I asked, spreading my arms wide and imploring them for assistance.

Some stepped back, but most who remained got that look in their eyes. The one I was all too familiar with as I'd seen it in the mirror often enough.

It was a twinkle of anticipation, the surge of adrenaline, the chance to test your wits against something supernatural. It was game on.

As the air danced with magic of several kinds, the creature, a form neither solid nor truly spectral but somewhere between the two, heaved out of the hole, revealing its full size. It must have been fifteen feet at least, plus horns, and the capirote flattened as it hit the ceiling then sagged under the humidity fast dissipating because of the ungodly dry heat from beneath its feet.

It wasn't fast, these things seldom were, but what they lacked in speed they made up for with focus and general nastiness. It couldn't take you in its hand and down you went, it didn't work like that, but it could do something much worse. It could swallow your soul and destroy your body as your essence was ripped out. You'd be separated from your physical form, dead without visceral contact, and then off you went to some nasty realm of the Nolands, never to return.

But the power of the creature was often limited by the one who called it, and remote work like this was never as strong as the user imagined. I got the impression it was an amateur or someone not truly capable behind this, more a desperate attempt to track and stop me than anything. It was flickering, more like a hologram of a demon than a true calling of a creature with its power intact.

The Hounds? Nah, they'd do a better job, surely? Ah, just Nathan then? Yes, it would be him acting alone, a last-ditch effort to stop me.

As the wizards spread out evenly around the pool, and I joined them, we each called forth a ward and dragged our feet to the right, drawing an invisible line with a multitude of magical forces that erupted up into a barrier once the circle was complete. There were smiles and a few moans as those with little magic to spare began to waver.

It was now or never.

"Be gone, foul creature of the Nolands. You are not welcome."

"You are not welcome," came the chant taken up by those controlling the circle. We chanted over and over, and as the beast reached for me it pulled a clawed hand back sharply when a violent shockwave shook the magic circle that contained it. The demon jumped back, snarling.

"I have been promised many gifts if I take your pathetic life, human. You will be mine." With that, the creature breathed in deep and sprang up high.

My stomach dropped, thinking it would clear the circle and destroy us all. As it rose, a terrible chattering and clawing at my mind increased until I felt my sanity slip, overwhelmed with corrupted visions of its home world. Mixed in were its dreams and maybe even desires, the things promised it by another human. There was a glimpse of Nathan, sat on the grass with his ruined arm, soaked in sweat and clutching a small trinket he must have had on his person.

It was him all right, and he'd promised this low-level demon more than it could have ever imagined. Items its kind would kowtow to, giving it power and position in its netherworld.

"Not today, and don't you know that hat's way past being stylish." I shot out my right arm and an invisible tendril of magic lassoed its leg. I clenched my fist, yanking the ephemeral line as the demon reached the top of its trajectory.

It bounced back then slammed down hard onto the pool floor, eliciting a groan from the Turk as the floor was utterly destroyed. I shouted, "Shrink the circle," and we all pushed out with our hands, forcing the invisible line off the edge of the pool and down to the shattered tiles below.

With the beast already getting to its feet, we shoved harder and the barrier contracted until the thing had no choice but to retreat. Even before we'd sent it back where it came from it flickered and wavered wildly, the strength needed to maintain such a summoning and control the creature's presence too much for Nathan to manage.

It blinked out of existence.

I sank to the scalding tiles amid cheers and shouts and high-fives, fist-bumping those that came to me to slap me on the back.

You'd think everyone would be shouting and carrying on, giving me grief and moaning, but they lived for this stuff, and a distraction was always welcome.

And besides, compared to some of the things that had gone on here it was pretty tame, just the final, foolhardy act of a man who'd lost. Nathan was alive, though, and I wasn't sure that was a good thing or a very bad thing.

But this smacked of desperation. It meant he hadn't reported to his superiors yet, and that meant he was in trouble for failing.

That, at least, gave me a little time. No more Hounds on my trail for a while, and Nathan was spent.

I got to my feet and apologized to the room and to the Turk especially. Everyone but him just smiled and began talking about the incident and reminiscing about all the other nasties that had come here over the years or had been conjured and got out of control.

One thing you can say about Satan's Breath, it ain't like any other sauna you'll ever visit.

"You still owe the Turk for the floor," said the Turk with a grumble, before he winked and I left to go get dressed.

Night Sweats

Demons notwithstanding, I felt rather refreshed once the cool night air hit. It was late now, gone two in the morning. The time I felt most alive, the time of magic. Of mystery.

I wished I could sleep at nights. I knew it would make me an entirely different person. Maybe even put a stop to the things I got involved in, but sleep hardly ever came in the dark, and it wasn't for lack of trying.

Maybe I was just scared. I knew too much, had seen too much, to find it easy to rest when the sun gave up its raging battle across the sky and the dark, cold night revealed the way to the stars. It's intimidating, the night sky. Makes you understand your position in the universe, how tiny and meaningless you are. That the power I drew on was what made everything I saw, and a lot I never would, endless, timeless. Enduring. And scary.

It's not the truth, though. It wasn't the wildness of the universe that scared me, it was the wildness of the hearts and minds of man that truly terrified me.

I'd never been a good sleeper, always tossed and turned and got up to mischief in the dark hours more often than not, but when George came into my life it escalated to a whole other level.

It was fear for her that tipped me over the edge into full-blown insomnia. I would lie awake, listening to the house, listening to the universe, listening for the evil intentions of men. I knew nobody could get into my house, knew she was safe, but it didn't matter. She had to be protected, so I would wait, and listen, and worry, and panic, and then I would get up and I would leave.

A contradiction, wanting to protect her, needing to, but leaving her alone. Not really. The house was safe, she was old enough to be left alone, and I was making life worse for us both by raging through the night in a restless semi-stupor.

So I went out and stole more stuff. It was cathartic. The rush of adrenaline, the fear, the tightness in my belly as I got close, and then the lifting of my spirits as I got away with it and finally the rush as I was paid.

I would return early in the morning, chipper and chatting, and I'd remain happy and content even as she moped about and moaned about the cereal or never even got out of bed until I had to crash and sleep for a few hours.

What can I say? I tried my best yet knew it wasn't good enough, that I should be there now to protect her from the bad men, but the bad men wouldn't harm her as they couldn't get in.

I drank in the darkness and the frigid air, feeling the coolness on my face, my lips tingling. But the rest of me was still warm from the sauna and the action, and my body was surging with the high of battle and the rush of endorphins.

One thing I knew was that I had to get on this and find a way to overcome the vampires. But it wasn't that easy. Short of decapitating every one of them there wasn't much that would stop them. And I doubted they'd be up for me doing that. I lacked information on them, on how they operated. More importantly, I lacked knowledge about Mikalus and how he could be resurrected.

With a sigh, knowing I had little choice if I was to succeed, and wondering if it was time anyway, I got in the car and drove to see someone who I knew would be pleased to see me no matter the time, day or night.

She was a night owl like me, and she would be up for this in her usual, infuriatingly happy and keen way.

I went to call on Vicky.

Geeky Gibberish

I tapped at the perfectly clean basement window and then cupped my hands to see if Vicky was in there. She was. Hunched over her computer, clacking away furiously like her life depended on it. I tapped again and she turned, rubbed her eyes, then sauntered over to the window.

I smiled and her almost childlike face lit up.

A moment later, I was walking through the door of a basement in a house in suburbia right out of the Stepford Wives. She closed it quickly behind me, locked it, before dashing back to her computer, whispering, "Sorry, be with you in a moment. Pour us some coffee, you look like you need it."

"Okay, Vicky, sure thing," I said, moving over to the small workbench against the wall with relish. I took in the aroma of coffee as I grabbed two mugs, one with World's Best Mum on it, the other one reading I'm A Mug, Get Over It. I bought her that one. Cool, eh?

Taking the jug off the heater, I poured us two large mugs of delightfully aromatic filter coffee.

Apparently, she put spices in it and used a blend of three beans. It tasted like heaven. Vicky was like that. Everything she did she did well, and everything she did she made her own. Mastered it. And most of what Vicky did drove her absolutely out of her mind with boredom.

"How's the slug?" I asked, tense muscles relaxing as the hot coffee tickled my taste buds and made everything all right in the world for a moment.

"Arthur!"

"Sorry."

"Don't be, he's making me crazy," said Vicky, pressing Enter with an unnecessary flourish then turning in her chair and taking the coffee I passed her.

"You look tired," I said, and she did. Her hair was pulled back tight in a perfect ponytail as always, and she had a little makeup on. Vicky would never be seen without it even if she was wearing her pink dressing gown and bunny slippers at two in the morning—you never knew if somebody like me might call—but she looked drawn, a darkness around her eyes and her forehead slightly wrinkled. Not that I'd ever mention the wrinkles, of course. I may have been stupid but not that stupid.

"I'm fine," she said, gulping her coffee.

"You lost weight again?" I asked, trying not to make it sound like an accusation. Hey, we all have our issues, and Vicky, perfect wife and mother though she was, was certainly no exception.

"I'm trying, but it's difficult."

"I know, honey, I know. For me, for the kids, even for the slug, just make sure you eat enough, okay?"

"Yes, Dad, will do."

Vicky had been petite and slender her whole life, but she drove herself too hard. She had a fast metabolism and an even faster brain, and she was trapped. Trapped in a loveless marriage to a man who spent his life with his phone glued to his ear. He was one of those overweight men that carried it badly—weak handshake and weaker morals—and he didn't deserve Vicky. I'm not sure anyone did. She was a nice lady, but a handful, and rather impulsive, but kind, and sweet, just, er, how to put this? Mad as a box of lobotomized frogs.

She had two kids she doted on and pretty much ran her household single-handed. She fed her family, cleaned up after them, washed dishes and did laundry. Went to PTA meetings, ran the children about in her Prius, even listened to her husband drone on about work endlessly when he was at home, and she did it all for love. Or some of it.

Vicky did what she thought right for her family, her children, and I was in absolutely no position to judge as my faults far outweighed hers in ways too numerous to list.

She also struggled with eating disorders because of her obsessive and compulsive nature. She forgot to eat, then binged, then freaked about eating too much, then got stable for a while before slipping back into bad habits and losing an unhealthy amount of weight all over again. Then Vicky panicked and ate more and then worried if she could pinch a little skin at her belly and proceeded to crash diet. It was tough for her, but she tried, and every year she spent longer with a handle on it.

I don't know how many times I'd told her that a little extra weight was a nice thing, that being soft and curvy was attractive and desirable, but it was stupid and pointless. She knew these things, understood what she did and why, but that's not why we do extreme things in our lives, is it? It isn't out of ignorance, it's because we all have weird crap in our head and we just muddle through, trying our best, aiming to be happy, sometimes succeeding, sometimes failing. Then, if we can, we pick ourselves up and go again the next day.

We drank in silence, rare when in Vicky's company, enjoying our coffee, both of us lost to our thoughts.

"Pepper's dead. He got shot this morning. He tried to kill me."

"Oh, goodie," said Vicky clapping her hands together with glee and spilling her coffee.

"Vicky! He was my friend, and he double-crossed me. Me! For money! Can you believe it?"

"I knew he was trouble. Eyes too close together. I told you, warned you. Shifty." She couldn't keep the smile off her face, and it was infectious even though entirely inappropriate.

"Don't look so happy about it. It ain't right."

Vicky ignored me and said, "So, can I be your sidekick now? Please. You said I could."

"I said no such thing," I protested. Vicky had been at me to be my sidekick for years. She wanted a way into this life and I didn't doubt would do anything short of disrupt the life of her kids to do it. She loved all this magic stuff, all the mystery, the excitement and danger, but deep down I always assumed she was joking, that it wasn't what she really wanted.

Or maybe it was. She certainly seemed keen to be my wingman. Wingwoman, sorry.

"You said I couldn't be your sidekick because you already had Pepper. Now you don't." She nibbled on her bottom lip.

Uh-oh.

"No, please don't. Vicky, anything but that."

It was too late, the tears began. I couldn't stand it when women cried. It did something to my insides and I felt helpless, like the worst kind of nasty, as if it was all my fault and I was a truly bad man.

I probably was. Maybe still am.

"Sorry, sorry. It's not that, it's... Oh, Arthur." Vicky sprang from her chair and launched her pint-sized body at me. She clung tight and I wrapped my arms around her, scared I'd break her. But she was strong and muscular from all her activities and the exercises she did religiously in the living room in in front of the TV every morning. What she called her "Me time," but I still worried I'd crush her.

"Hey, it's okay. What's the matter? Why so sad?"

She wriggled from my arms and stepped back. "Oh, it's nothing. It's everything. I don't know. Life?

Maybe it's just life. I'm just passing time. What do I do? Nothing. Cook and clean and act like a taxi."

"You stop that right this minute. You do the most important thing in the world. You look after your kids."

"Maybe," she said, pulling a tissue from up her sleeve. Why she always had a tissue up her sleeve was a mystery I knew I'd never solve. I asked her once and she just stared at me like I was an utter idiot. "In case I need it," was her answer. Can't argue with that. Especially not with Vicky.

"Hey, come on. Dry those eyes. I have something that'll cheer you up," I said, smiling even though inside all I felt was dread as the night wore on and I'd not even begun to deal with the rather pressing problem of a resurrected vampire.

"Sorry, I'm being silly. What is it? Something gross?"

Vicky did like the gross stuff. "Very," I said. "What do you know about Mikalus' ashes, or Mikalus in general?"

"Oh my God, oh my God! You found them, didn't you? I knew you were good. I can't believe it, this is so awesome. He's like the most powerful, dangerous vampire there has ever been. The first vampire to walk the earth, a real monster. He's the only one that can bring them back from the weak position they now hold. They dwindle year on year and become less and less effective and there's no way that can change without him being resurrected. Can I see? Can I see?" Vicky was falling over herself with excitement. Babbling non-stop and making what I had to say next even harder.

"Um, I gave the ashes to the vampires." That put a damper on the situation, and then some.

"You utter idiot."

"I know."

"You've doomed us all."

"I know, all right?" I said, exasperated. "Still, beats being bored, right?" And with that we burst out laughing.

Maybe it was the coffee.

A Temporary Arrangement

I filled a very excitable Vicky in on what exactly had gone down and my thoughts on the whole sorry mess. The latter didn't take long, mainly because I had none beyond "Ugh."

"Okay, wait. Let me make sure I have this straight. You planned to give the ashes to Nigel, but Nigel's brother shot him because he knew Nigel was going to give them to the vampires?"

"Yes."

"Then this Nathan told you they both worked for Cerberus, and that they'd tried to kill you, too, to get the ashes?"

"Yes, kind of. Look, he didn't tell me what I had. If he'd just done that then none of this would have happened."

"So why didn't he?"

"Dunno. Guess he figured I was a bad guy and wouldn't hand it over if I knew. He seemed panicked, now I think about it. Not outwardly, but if he sent that lesser demon to try to get rid of me, you can bet he was working alone. It was a pretty lame attempt, especially for the Hounds. I reckon he's been out on his own on this one, found out about his brother, freaked, called a few people to deal with it, and then hopped on a train or whatever and got here as fast as he could."

"Why not tell his fellow Hounds? And that's such a stupid name."

"I know, right? As to why all the secrecy, who knows? Maybe he just wanted it kept quiet. Save his brother's, and his, reputation, I guess. And when the goons failed to get me he came himself, just to make sure. But that blew up in his face, too, and my guess is that now he's desperate and will be running out of time. Cerberus will have heard about Nigel, it was pretty messy, so Nathan will be in deep shit if he doesn't give a good explanation. Either he tells them what's happened, or he'll do something desperate to get me out of principle."

"What about Sasha, does she know?" Vicky smiled at the mention of Sasha. They'd met a few times over the years, and although Vicky took some convincing about the whole faery godmother thing, she couldn't really ignore the fact Sasha could just turn up wherever she wanted. It was only her sense of politeness that made her act even remotely human.

"Ugh, I haven't told her, if that's what you mean." Damn, she wouldn't be happy. Fae and vamps had never been the best of friends, and this certainly complicated things no end. Sasha knew what went on in the world of mortals, but was very choosy about what she helped me with or said. Something to do with the whole interfering in mortal affairs thing, with a bit of time-travel-like danger of paradox thrown in. She explained it to me a few times but it just made my head hurt.

She could only interfere if she knew she'd interfered, as that meant there would be no paradox. Could only tell me what she knew she was supposed to. Her home world was not ours, and time was very different for the fae. They were on their own particular timeline, where the ages meant little and to them our world was nothing but a distraction, hardly even real. So although they could come and mess about, there were limits imposed because this wasn't their home. Where the line was drawn I had no idea. Whenever she tried to explain the difference, the way things were, it ended up being like trying to explain the concept of flying to a fish. It was another world outside of my experience, and the concepts didn't compute even a little.

"I know everything," said Sasha from the doorway, now open even though I knew for a fact Vicky had locked it.

"Hey, Sasha, how you doing?" I asked, hoping she'd come to help not to scold.

"Sasha!" said Vicky, up out of her chair in a flash, ushering Sasha in, closing and locking the door behind her.

They hugged, holding it a little too long for me to feel comfortable, and their hands were placed a little too low, and were a little too excited, for me to feel comfortable either. I've often wondered if... Nah, just my overactive imagination, I'm sure.

"You gave the ashes of the First to the vampires, didn't you?" said Sasha, waggling her finger at me in accusation.

I winced, and kept trying to lean away from her finger. It'd been known to go off and do terrible things and she sure as hell didn't need a wand to make you very dead very fast.

"Hey, I didn't know. A heads-up would've been nice."

"Oh, I'm sorry, I didn't realize I was faery godmother to an ape. I thought The Hat was a wizard. I didn't for one moment think he was a person who could carry around the ashes of the most famous vampire in history without knowing."

"I—"

"Do not interrupt!" warned Sasha, her brow creasing. Trust me, when something as beautiful as a faery brow creases you shut the hell up, do the zipper motion, then throw away the key.

"And, I didn't realize he could walk into the den of the only remaining vampires of any power in the country and hand over said ashes without considering maybe it wasn't a good idea."

"You had to be there," I mumbled. It was rather harsh but she did have a point, I guess.

"Okay, your idiocy aside, what did you want? I'm busy, got a date."

"A date? With who?" I asked, suddenly feeling paternal and wondering if her date had a good job and sound prospects. Yes, I'm fully aware of the pot calling the kettle black, thank you very much.

"None of your business!" snapped Sasha before she brushed past me, seemingly in a mood for some reason, then checked her hair and make-up in the reflection on the monitor screen.

Vicky said, "You look beautiful."

"Thank you, my dear. See, Arthur, some people have manners."

"You do look beautiful, as always. I just, er, didn't know fae had dates."

"How do you think we meet men and have sex, then?" asked Sasha, head cocked to the side, body wrapped up tight in sheer fabric that left just about nothing to the imagination. I got that funny feeling again, the one that made me utterly discombobulated. I knew she wasn't a relation, but she was my faery godmother, so having those kind of thoughts messed with my head no end.

"Don't talk about sex, it confuses me," I said, putting my hands in my ears.

Sasha spoke and put her hands on her hips, waiting.

"Sorry, couldn't hear you," I said, removing my fingers.

"I said, it's easy once you get the hang of it."

"Huh? What are you talking about? Oh, no, I didn't mean sex confuses me. Although, er, I suppose it does. No, I meant thinking of you having sex is... Damn, can we change the subject?"

"How about a cuppa?" asked Vicky, fawning over Sasha.

"Sorry, gotta dash. My date is very hot, and I mean literally." Sasha winked at Vicky and they shared a laugh together. I had absolutely no idea what they were laughing at but didn't ask. I knew better.

"Why did you come?" I asked.

"To say hello to Vicky."

"Aw, that's so sweet."

"My pleasure," said Sasha, smiling a gorgeous smile. "Ah, almost forgot. And to warn you. Fix this, or the vampires will be the least of your worries." Sasha was serious, just about every magic user on the planet, plus plenty of true preternatural creatures, would be out for my blood if I brought about the rise of the vampires after so long without them being more than a footnote to history.

"I'm trying to fix things," I protested. "If all these damn government spooks, Hounds, whatever, and the rest didn't keep getting in the way it would make my life a lot easier."

"Excuses, excuses," said Sasha with a tut. She was an expert tutter, had medals, I was sure.

"I know, right?" agreed Vicky.

"Get Vicky here to help."

I stared at Sasha to see if she was trying to be funny or not. I had no idea. "Why do you think I'm here?"

"I mean take her with you to help. You need a new sidekick."

"That's what I said," squawked Vicky, practically packing her bag for the fun vampire infiltration outing.

"No way, she has kids. She'll get hurt."

"You have a kid. You'll get hurt. You do get hurt," said Vicky as if stating the obvious to a child. "You still do it, though."

"That's different," I said, knowing it was lame.

"It isn't," said Sasha, and with a wink to Vicky she was gone in a sparkle of faery dust. I'm sure she made dramatic exits just to impress Vicky. When she was with me she walked or drove away like a normal person.

"Ha!" said Vicky.

"Ugh," said I.

Sometimes, I was sure there were too many women in my life. Women of the wrong sort. Meaning, women that refused to treat me with anything approaching respect and seemed to delight in abusing me and making my life more difficult. It's the hat, or the trousers, or something.

To Work

"Okay, look, you can tag along if you want, but won't it be awkward, what with the kids and all?" I was hoping I could guilt Vicky into changing her mind about becoming my temporary sidekick. Pepper's death weighed heavily and I didn't want her in danger. She was tough, but had no idea what it was really like out in the wilds where people would chew up and spit out daydreaming moms without a second thought. She'd tagged along plenty of times before, but not when there was anything to actually worry about.

"Really, you mean it?" Vicky performed a cringeworthy mom dance but I smiled and turned away lest it put me off her for life.

"You shouldn't do that, you know," I said, talking to the wall.

"What, this?"

Resigned, I turned to watch as Vicky gyrated her hips and did a weird rolling motion with her arms. Looking like the demented, sleep-deprived, exhausted and lonely insomniac that she was. Her movements got faster and faster.

Then the inevitable happened.

"Ugh, it burns, it burns." It was too late. The belt on the heavy dressing gown came undone and the fabric parted. She had nothing on and, I have to admit, she was a lot rounder and curvier than I'd ever imagined. I'd assumed she'd be skin and bone, but the gal had curves.

"Haha, you big baby. Oops, haha." Vicky blushed in that cute way of hers, but seemed rather brazen if you ask me. Showed a side of herself I was rather surprised at. She sorted herself out and thankfully the dancing was at an end.

"Enough messing about. If I don't deal with this and come up with something then life won't be worth living. I need information, and I need it fast."

"Then we go fight vampires?" asked my diminutive sidekick with utter, unbridled glee.

"Yeah, then we go fight vampires," I agreed, with about as much enthusiasm as a man being given the last rites. I was playing it down a little to calm Vicky, but this was serious and she had to understand the risks. I hadn't lost hope, though, wouldn't until I breathed my last. Even then, I knew I'd keep on trying even if I had to battle the vampires from some nasty hell for wayward wizards.

Vicky sat at what she liked to call her office chair, when in fact this was no office. It was a smelly basement rammed with tins of paint and the assorted detritus accumulated over years of living in the burbs.

She had a tiny desk with a good quality chair because she spent every spare moment she could in here, which, with her busy life chasing about after her family, meant she usually came down after everyone else was sleeping soundly.

Vicky found it hard to sleep, same as me. Although not a true insomniac, years of being a mother had forced her to cope on little sleep. The extended deprivation had resulted in her being restless most nights, so she turned to something creative and became what many would call rather black hat with her computer activities.

This slight, immaculately made-up, prim, bolshy and bossy mother of two, and my friend, was a hacker. She did it for fun, so she said, and never did anything that would hurt anyone else, but I knew her skills had grown to be considerable over time. I also knew she'd used said skills to hack into the school she had chosen for her girls, and with some careful manipulations of the records had seen to it that her kids were accepted. I didn't doubt she'd made plenty of other tweaks over the years to if not outright steal then to certainly make life go in the direction she thought best.

"Okay, what do you need?" She cracked her fingers and then her hands hovered over the keyboard, eyes glazed and already in the zone. Expectant and waiting for the adventure to begin.

"I need everything you can find on Mikalus and what happened to him. The state of the vampire community in the country now, and worldwide, and I need to know how they plan on resurrecting him. And you need to be quick, as I don't know how long we have left."

I wondered how long the hole would take to burn through my head, deciding it wouldn't be long judging by the intensity of the gaze Vicky leveled on me. "What? Why are you looking at me like that?"

"You mean to tell me you gave them the ashes, they want to resurrect Mikalus, and you didn't try to stop them right away and you don't know whether or not they're right now bringing him back from the dead? What if they've done it already?"

"You are such a noob."

"Am not!"

"Are too."

"I'll open my dressing gown again. And do my dancing," Vicky threatened as she moved to stand.

"No, okay, I'll talk, haha."

"That's my boy."

Somehow, within the last five minutes or so, I seemed to have lost my power of authority. I would be reduced to sidekick status if I didn't get my act together. Vicky had that effect on people. She took charge, was a whirlwind, and it could leave you dazed and confused, wondering what the hell just happened unless you kept a careful eye on what she did and made you do before you even realized it.

"They won't do anything in a hurry or half-arsed, it's too important. Nigel wouldn't have made arrangements to hand it over until he was sure he had it first. They must have been keeping a close eye on me, or him, making sure everything went smoothly, and when it didn't they jumped in and played it by ear, same as everyone else."

"So what? They could still be resurrecting him right now."

"Nah, you know what they're like. Gotta have rituals and all that good stuff. Actually, it isn't optional. They will need seriously strong magic for this, and there will be rules. A resurrection is almost impossible at the best of times. How many necromancers do you know?"

"Um, none."

"Exactly! So—"

"But I don't know anyone who uses magic apart from you," interrupted Vicky.

"Um, yes, well, you know what I mean. Black magic is hard, and scary, and you can't just chuck a bucket of blood at the ashes of a long dead vampire and BAM, he's back. It takes time, lots of time. There will be cleansing rituals, all that good stuff. I know the basics of these things, just not the specifics for someone like Mikalus. It'll take hours even if they were ready to go immediately. So, get to it and find out what they'll do and how long we have left."

"Yes sir." Vicky saluted and got to work.

I drank coffee and thought about my options. It didn't take long; I didn't have many.

A Plan (Kinda)

Vicky's nimble fingers flew across the keyboard faster than a vampire to a blood buffet and just as keen. She set up some kind of bot that would trawl places not accessible via regular search engines, the more secretive and unlisted private networks used by universities and institutions more likely to have research or downright speculation on the more arcane stuff. Pity there was no wizard intranet, but it was a surefire way to get into trouble, fast. The powers-that-be absolutely refused to allow the knowledge gathered over millennia to be digitized.

It always surprised me how much stuff was hidden in this digital mire, and Vicky'd told me there was more information in these private networks for governments, libraries, corporations and the like than in what most of us thought of as the World Wide Web. But the moment she started talking about Tor and Onion networks and how to access these places using proxy servers my eyes glazed over and I lost focus. I'd mumble appropriate sounds but understood none of it. I may have been black hat, but not in this digital world.

Anyway, it didn't take her long to get the information. There was a surprising amount of written work based around the vampires, much of it little more than fairy tales, but some of it was seriously old, and some of it was damn close to the mark. There were books, private and secret books, that had been kept under wraps but could be accessed if you had a computer genius like Vicky, as the pages were always either scanned into a system somewhere or painstakingly copied out to be sure they were preserved for posterity. Rare, but it was there.

Vicky accessed several such ancient tomes, ones I'd heard of but never read. Most of the really important stuff, though, the truth behind the myths, could never be accessed this way. It was too important, too well hidden, too dangerous to be known about by scholars unschooled in magic. My work meant I'd seen enough important books over the years to know they were too powerful to ever see the light of day. Passed down over the ages, kept secret and the information shared only with a select few, but she did what she could, and it was enough.

"The Book of Mikalus," she said as she brought up a frighteningly long piece of work. The musings of a now deceased professor who'd uncovered a book thought lost that mysteriously disappeared once he'd managed to read it. It concerned the resurrection of the fabled original vampire, and this dude had written extensively on the book he'd read, what he could remember. It droned on and on, mostly with a wry amusement that the authors clearly seemed to believe it was the truth.

"Think this is about as good as we're gonna get," I said. "And we need to get going. Give me the gist of it, how they can do it." I tried to read what was on the screen, but Vicky was one fast reader, and she scanned through the endless pages too quickly for me. Then she got exasperated and threw up a few search queries and sat back while the computer did its work. Whittling the endless waffle down to a more manageable size.

After an intolerable amount of time listening to her mumbling as she speed-read the relevant pages, she finally sat back and said, "Seems like you were right. It'll take a while."

"Good. I've heard the basics, of how they do it. Something to do with a blood sacrifice, and lots of the usual washing and donning of cool robes, all that kinda stuff. What's the real deal?"

"This professor, and this is just what he could remember, said the book talked about the ten. Ten true Children of Blood. The blood children of Mikalus."

"Okay, that'll mean Seconds. His firstborn, so to speak. What else?"

"Most of it's kind of nonsensical. Even he had a hard job making much sense of it. He talks about the blood of the ten needed to resurrect Mikalus, that it has to touch what remains, and then there's this." Vicky pointed at the screen where she'd highlighted a paragraph. "It's about the only passage he could actually remember properly, probably as it's the most important."

I leaned forward and read, "And you shall be cleansed by the pure one, unsullied and touched by the universe."

"What does that mean?" asked Vicky, looking at me like I'd have the answer.

"Not sure. Does the Prof say who this was directed at?"

"Hang on." Vicky clicked about a few times, going back and forth, and said, "Well, the whole book is like a guide for those that would resurrect Mikalus. It's written for the ten. So this is telling them they need to be cleansed by this pure one. What does touched by the universe mean?"

I stood, back aching from leaning forward. "No idea. Touched by the universe. Unsullied. All those words could be the wrong translation, or they could mean something different back then. Not that I know what they mean now. Okay, enough of this. Go get dressed, it's time to leave." If I'd thought I could have changed her mind I would have tried, but I knew when I was beat.

"You got a plan?" Vicky was practically ready to run out the door, dressing gown gaping.

"I do. But you won't like it."

"How do you know?"

"Because I sure as hell don't."

Vicky smiled at me then ran up the stairs to go creep about and prepare to go hunting vampires. This would not go well at all.

Bit Obvious

The drive was surprisingly quiet, meaning Vicky stopped to breathe now and then. I tried to warn her about Merrick, the guy we were going to see, but she just smiled that mom smile of hers, like I was talking about a bully at school and not to worry as the adults were here now.

When she was like this I never knew whether to be terrified for her life, or pleased she still had such faith in the world. That she could look to the positive in all things, including gangsters that ran the city and were utterly ruthless. Some of the criminals I dealt with were nice people, did things outside the law but would rather chop off their own arm than hurt another human being. Merrick would rather chop your arm off and then hurt you some more.

He dealt in the darker side of life, where violence and intimidation were how things got done, and he was good at it. He'd risen to the top years ago and stayed there. A thug, pure and simple, but treated it like a business and acted accordingly.

Although I knew he lived in a swanky house in an exclusive part of the city, he conducted business, and much of that was nocturnal, out of an abandoned Victorian house that stood alone, surrounded by nothing but demolished dreams and broken concrete. A redevelopment halted before it even got started. He owned it, of course, bought it for a song when the developer went bust, and would hold on to it until land prices rose enough to satisfy him.

In the meantime, he used it as his base of operations since it gave off a suitably "street" vibe to impress the younger crowd and the poverty-stricken who understood such a world. The atmosphere of decay solidified the image they had of him—he was like them, brought up with nothing and clawed his way out of the gutter through crime.

Nothing could have been further from the truth. Merrick was university educated and smart, but found the criminal life paid better than the white collar jobs he'd tried and shunned in his early twenties.

He had strict standards and stricter punishments, and going to see him was a bad idea. But he was the only person who might have what I needed. I may have been a criminal but I didn't exactly get on with the more violent types, mainly because they kept getting themselves killed and I couldn't stomach even looking at them.

"We're here," I said to Vicky as I pulled up alongside several gleaming black SUVs, totally out of place beside the graffiti-covered house. It had a good roof, but most windows were smashed and it was covered in ivy. Perfect for an evil overlord to unnerve his employees and those he wanted something from.

"I've never met a proper gangster before, not like Merrick." Vicky was buzzing, all twitchy and excited. Did this woman have no fear?

"Just act normal and don't say anything stupid." I thought for a moment then added, "No, don't act normal. Be quiet and don't talk unless spoken to."

"Whatever you say," said Vicky brightly, hopping out the car before I had chance to calm her down a little more.

We entered through the missing front door, the goon eyeing us with malefic intent. He was good, proper menacing, even had a grunt and everything. Vicky smiled her winning smile at him then straightened his tie and waggled her finger at him. What could I do? She hadn't spoken yet so was keeping her word.

Damn, but if he didn't bow his head, look chastised and mumble, "Sorry."

She had this way about her, like your mum was telling you off. Didn't matter if you were a hardened goon or one of her kids, the result was always the same. You knew you were in the presence of a true force of nature and didn't want to disappoint her.

Outside the door that led to Merrick's lair, another goon grunted at us and told us to wait while he knocked then went inside to announce us. A few seconds later he came out, glared at us then mumbled "In," and stepped aside.

A Close Shave

The office was clean, ordered, minimal. The lighting was clever, angled to highlight Merrick and Brains in a way that created deep shadow, making them seem large and the focus of attention. It pointed away from them slightly so it glared, making it harder to attack, if that was what you had in mind. Apart from the office desk the room contained a sofa and coffee table, a large TV, a wall of neatly aligned books, and little else. The floor was ancient floorboards covered in a large rug, and they creaked as we walked from the shadows into the light.

"Look here, Brains, it's the wizard. Haha." Merrick wiped his face with a towel and leaned back in his chair. His gangster chair. Oversized and covered in expensive leather. He put his hands behind his head, a flash of expensive watch revealed as his cuffs rode up. He was clearly amused. For about a second, then his smile vanished, his expression cold, and hard.

In usual fashion, he changed position. It was a strange mannerism, but he never seemed to stay still for a moment. It made you wonder what he was about to do, and the guns on the table didn't help to ease your concerns. He leaned forward, adjusted his narrow black tie, dark as his shirt and his soul, and buffed a cuff link I knew for a fact was worth more than most folks earned in a year. I should know, I gave them to him in exchange for a book he thought was of no value, but made me very rich, and helped Vicky out of a tight spot when their house flooded and the insurance didn't pay up.

"Wizard," said Merrick again, trying to make light of it. He didn't fool me, the whole idea made him nervous because he knew it was real but couldn't quite get the information to compute in the right way.

"Haha," responded Brains on cue, his slender frame immobile, the laughter about as genuine as his interest in me. He was such a sycophant. It made me sick when people played up to others just to ingratiate themselves. But Brains had been the, er, brains of Merrick's operation for many years, and there were rumors that their constant companionship went beyond mere work and was much closer and more intimate.

Which would be fine, but it meant I had to be careful what I said to Brains as well as Merrick. Insult one and you insulted both, and getting on the wrong side of Merrick was a very, very bad idea.

Merrick outright loved magic, was a believer in his own special way, but he still found it immensely amusing that I called myself a wizard and had a wand. To him, the whole magic thing was one big ball of confusion. He was one of those people that got it, believed what I did was something unique and harnessed the powers of the universe in unknowable and strange ways. But it was still magic to him, if that makes sense?

Almost like when you see a magician do something and you know what you see isn't possible and that it's a trick. Merrick was like that. He believed what he had seen really happened, but didn't truly believe. Like I and others with similar, although obviously less refined, skills had some secret we kept hidden. A trick, in other words.

"Hi, Merrick. Brains."

"Arthur 'The Hat' Salzman, it's been too long. How you been?" asked Merrick as he studied me carefully. Merrick may have acted like just another gangster, but he wasn't. It was all a front, a performance. Sure, he had his guys, his goons, but he, and most of them, were a breed apart. Intelligent, sharp, fingers on the pulse of the city and the country as a whole. He was an intelligent man, but hid it. It gave him an advantage. Many people had underestimated Merrick over the years, and most of them were dead and in very tiny chunks.

He was a solid looking guy, well-fed but far from overweight. A presence. He dressed in black as that's what gangsters did, and his people wore variations of the same outfit. He liked the order, the military aspect, and much as I hated to admit it, the style made an impression—it scared you.

"Oh, you know. Alive." I adjusted my hat, tilted it back a little so I looked open and friendly, nothing to hide. Or I tried. But Merrick was a keen observer of body language. He knew your next move and had the look of the predator beneath his fake smile.

"And who's the straight? You got yourself a housewife for a girl? You know adultery is bad, right?"

"I'm not his girl. I'll have you know I'm happily married," said Vicky as she stepped forward and squared her tiny shoulders. Being dressed in her usual uninspired clothes probably didn't help her seem very intimidating, but not a lot would. "Er, well, I'm married, anyway."

"Haha, I like her, Arthur. She's got some spirit."

"And you need a new barber," said Vicky. We watched as a nervous man in his twenties who Merrick had brushed aside when we entered now returned to his work. One of the new, tattooed hairdressers that seemed to have sprung up everywhere and catered to those who liked a neat, trimmed beard and were willing to pay to have it maintained.

He lathered up Merrick again then began when Merrick tilted back his head and grunted permission. The barber's hands shook as he used a cutthroat razor to shave the muscular neck. No easy task at the best of times, but Merrick had a reputation and it made folks nervous.

"Ow, shit." Merrick pulled back and wiped at his neck, blood and shaving foam glinting in the light as he inspected his finger. He glared at the barber who spluttered an apology and was sweating badly.

"Told you," said Vicky, looking way too smug.

"What, you think you can do better, little Miss Tiny?"

Before I could grab her, Vicky marched forward right up to the chair and got way closer to Merrick than I would have recommended.

"Try me. I don't get nervous. I'm a gangster, too."

When the laughter died down, which took a while, Merrick said, "Damn, but she's funny."

"She's just tired, Merrick, don't worry about her. Can we talk? I have business I think you'll be interested in."

Merrick waved away my words and said, "Okay, gangster lady, show me." He turned to the nervous barber and said, "Get lost." The guy practically ran out the room, leaving his gear behind.

"Now, come on, Merrick, she was just joking. She might cut you, and nobody wants that."

"Arthur, you come in here with this little Stepford mom and she gives me no end of lip. If," he held up a finger, nail perfectly manicured, "she cuts me then it will not be good. She wants to be a player, fine."

"And if I don't?" asked Vicky.

"Quiet, Vicky," I warned.

"Relax, Arthur, I used to shave Dad when I was a little girl. It's easy." Vicky turned back to Merrick and said, "If I don't cut you, then you'll listen to Arthur and do what he asks?"

"Sure thing, Mom. Don't cut me," he warned.

The next five minutes were a lesson in what it truly meant to have nerves of steel. Vicky lathered up Merrick, sharpened the blade expertly, and set to work with practiced strokes. She talked non-stop, chastised Merrick about the condition of his skin, recommended products to improve the look of his beard, commented on his aftershave, and asked him to tilt his head when needed. Even pushed his chin up when he was slow to comply.

At first, Merrick was all grunts and conspiratorial winks at Brains. He kept fidgeting—on purpose—to make Vicky nervous so she'd cut him a little. But she didn't, and soon he relaxed and they chatted like they were old friends.

She had a way about her, that's for sure. And if she'd had balls, they would be made of pure, shiny steel.

"Finished," said Vicky as she wiped down Merrick and cleaned up the gear.

Merrick ran a hand over his neck and smartly trimmed beard, then took the mirror Brains offered him and asked, "What do you think? Feels damn smooth and looks all right."

"She did a great job," said Brains. "Real pro." He took the mirror back.

Vicky came to stand back beside me, and Merrick leaned forward in his chair. "You've got a good hand. Good eye, too. Let me ask you something."

"Sure," said Vicky looking calm, but I could tell she was tense by the way she kept wiggling her fingers behind her back.

"How come you never paused at the scars, or got nervous? You know I'm bad, right?"

"Mr. Merrick, I am a mother of two children and a wife to a fat man. I have seen more gross stuff, wiped more backsides, seen more puke, tended more wounds, inspected more weird lumps and dealt with more crying and tantrums than I care to remember. And that's just my husband. If you think a little scarring on your neck and face will make me nervous then you underestimate me."

"Haha. I think you're right. I like you..."

"Vicky."

"I like you, Vicky, and I'm true to my word. What can I do for you, Arthur, and Vicky? You know what, we should call you the Barber. All good gangsters have a nickname."

"How about the Blade?" said Vicky, eyes shining. Damn, she'd always wanted a nickname, said it wasn't fair she never had one.

"Haha. Vicky, 'the Blade,' it is."

I'd never hear the last of this. But, I had to admit, she was pretty hardcore to remain so calm, especially dealing with Merrick and the mess that was his neck and jaw.

"Now, let's get down to business." Merrick nodded to Brains. He brought two chairs over and we sat the other side of the desk from Merrick. Brains remained standing beside him, ever vigilant, ever ready to do his master's bidding.

An Interruption

"Boss, Boss, did you hear about..." Chaz, one of Merrick's goons and a real piece of work, paused halfway across the room when he saw me. I gave him a cold stare, my most unfriendly, and then turned back to face Merrick.

Merrick frowned and his face darkened. "What the fuck have I told you about barging in without knocking? If I wanted this place to be a zoo I'd hire monkeys. Are you a monkey, Chaz? Is that what it is? You've turned into a baboon or a gorilla?"

"Actually, they aren't all monkeys," said Vicky. "They're—"

"Quiet," I whispered to her. She saw sense and shut the hell up. Maybe there was hope for her yet. Maybe.

"Sorry, Boss, just heard about our 'friend' here being involved in some real shit today and thought you should now."

"I know all about it. What do you think I am, an amateur? Get out of here, unless you want to get a shave. A real close shave?"

I turned to face Chaz, just so I could watch him squirm. He was an utter fool, cruel too, and I absolutely did not like him. I'd crossed his path before on many occasions, and we'd had words. He had it in for me, and I knew one day there would be a reckoning.

"No, sorry. But I wanna kill this guy." Chaz scowled at me and tried to give me a hard look.

"You got grit in your eye? You look like maybe you're having a seizure or something," I said, showing him what a real hard look was.

"I'll slice your throat and watch you bleed out." Chaz's fingers twitched as they hovered by his side where I knew he kept a vicious blade. It was his favorite thing, cutting people and taunting them as they died. Merrick was a hard man, brutal, but employing the likes of Chaz was still a strange choice. He didn't fit with the image Merrick went to great pains to convey, that of a gangster whose orders were obeyed without question, but I guess having wild goons kept the business running and the money flowing.

"Try it. I'll ram that little penknife of yours so far into your head I'm sure to hit that tiny pea in your skull you call a brain eventually."

"Why you..." Chaz stormed forward, knife already in hand, a cruel, angry sneer on his face. Eyes sparkling with the anticipation of watching my blood seep into the large and very expensive rug.

"You know what, Chaz," sighed Merrick, "sometimes I think you are a valuable asset. Other times, like now, I wonder what is wrong with me. I am conducting business with Arthur here, and his fine lady friend, the Blade," that got a smile from Vicky, "and you dare interrupt me over a stupid, petty rivalry you have with Arthur?"

"He stole my stuff. He took what I was due."

"I explained this to you, Merrick, you too, Chaz. You crossed the line and you messed with someone you knew better than to mess with." It's a long story, but suffice to say Chaz got rather carried away and did something he ought not to have done. Once the incident was over, I went straight to Merrick and explained the situation. He understood, Chaz got reprimanded, and he'd hated me ever since.

"And I thought I'd told you that Arthur here is our friend. Unless he crosses us."

"He's gonna get what's his."

With a huff, I got up. This had gone on long enough. Chaz was a sneak and I knew at some point he'd try to kill me in a cowardly way. It was a night for resolution, so what the hell? "If you give me permission, I'll deal with this now," I said to Merrick.

Merrick shrugged, looking amused. "It's your funeral. Chaz's pretty handy with a blade."

"And I'm a fucking wizard."

That brought laughter from the gangsters and a look of real worry from Vicky. The truth was, I had to do this. I knew Merrick doubted the truth about what I was capable of, and I needed him on side a hundred percent. Plus, I wanted to scare the living daylights out of Vicky so she'd understand the world she had asked to be a part of. Hopefully, she'd go home and stick to the computer.

"Haha, okay, wizard, you have my permission." Merrick leaned forward over his desk, keen to see what would happen.

"Time to say goodbye, Arthur," said Chaz, eye twitching nervously as he got more excited. "And when I'm done watching you bleed out I'm gonna take this little lady here and—"

Already half turned so I was facing Chaz, I lifted the warm rod already primed for action. As Chaz grinned manically, performing a slicing action with the knife in front of his throat in a demonstration of what he was going to do to me, I slashed the wand fast, cutting through the air with a whoosh and directing not inconsiderable force right at his arm, pushing it with immense power.

Chaz made a strange gaggling sound, then lifted the blade away from where it had been forced hard against his throat. He stared, unbelieving, as ruby blood dripped from the long, razor sharp blade. He bent his head and watched as his shirt stained red, the white cotton soaking up his blood like a sponge.

His head lifted, gaze resting on me. The wand was hot in my hand. A comfort. Grounding me and reminding me that the violence was over. I needed to calm down.

"Nobody threatens my friend like that." I turned away from him, sat back down in my chair, and locked eyes with Merrick. The lifeless body of Chaz toppled backward with a thud I ignored and I continued, "Now, can we please get back to our business?"

There was shocked silence. Vicky kept staring at me then the wand until I put it away. Brains remained motionless and impassive, and Merrick, well, he took a moment then a huge grin spread across his ravaged features.

"Damn, Arthur, you are one cold, hardcore dude."

"And a wizard," I reminded him, keeping my face relaxed even though all I wanted to do was throw up. I knew it was the only way, though. To show everyone in the room who I was, what I was, and to ensure everyone took this seriously. A lesson for Vicky, a proving of strength to Merrick, and a way to get the roach, Chaz, off my back once and for all.

What can I tell you? I knew it was wrong to kill, but I would not, would never, let anyone threaten those I cared about. It just wasn't gonna happen.

A Request

A few minutes later, nobody saying a word, Chaz's body was dragged out, the rug was rolled up and removed, and it was as if none of it had ever happened. I'd made my point, though, and knew it stood me in better stead with Merrick. A weird way to gain trust, but Merrick was no regular guy. You had to prove yourself, and this showed him I was willing to do what it took to get things done.

Vicky remained silent, but I knew it hadn't had the desired effect. She was hyper. Her fast breathing, the way her eyes shone, the bouncing of her leg, it all told me she was as high as a kite. I'd done a bad thing going to her.

"Enough games. What do you want, Arthur? Why have you come here at this ungodly hour and interrupted my peace?"

"I need a bazooka."

Merrick, and even Brains, spent the next few minutes laughing, which just wasn't nice. Once they'd calmed down, Merrick said, "Arthur, what makes you think I've got a bloody bazooka hanging about? Have you been watching cartoons or something? Nobody uses bazookas. This is England for fuck's sake! If you wanna blow something up why not use your magic?"

"Because time is of the essence and if I use my magic I won't have any left for what comes next."

"Oh, and what comes after you blow something up?"

"I have to kill vampires."

Merrick didn't laugh this time. My tone must have told him I was serious. "You're kidding me, right?"

"He's not. They're real and we have to stop them," said Vicky.

"Tonight," I added.

"You guys are killing me here. Vampires, this I gotta see."

"So, do you have a bazooka?"

"No, why would I?"

"Because I know you have guns, lots and lots of guns. Proper ones, machine guns, and I assumed you pretty much had an arsenal."

"Sorry to disappoint, but no, we don't. I've never liked guns. Way too easy for them to get into the wrong hands. Yes, we use them when necessary, but no, no secret stash of weapons, I'm afraid. Just the usual."

I said nothing about the guns on the table. Didn't seem to me like he hated them all that much. "And what's the usual?" This wasn't going as planned at all. It was time to leave. I'd wasted enough time already.

"Arthur, that's none of your business. Look, I'm not about to go blowing shit up with bazookas, that's nuts."

"Okay, thanks anyway. Guess we should be going." I could have kicked myself for the delay. All I'd done was drain myself and get sidetracked.

We got to our feet and moved to leave, but Brains bent and whispered in Merrick's ear.

"Really?" asked Merrick, looking surprised. "Well, imagine that."

Brains whispered something else and Merrick nodded then said, "Apparently, we do have something that could be of help."

"Oh?"

"Got a few grenades, if they'll do the job?"

"Yes!" shouted Vicky, and pulled my hand up and high-fived me before I could stop her.

I definitely hadn't turned her off the life of a gangster. The Blade was warming to the violence a little too readily.

Straight to It

Within minutes, I'd filled Merrick in on what I wanted done and given him the address. We waited while he spoke quietly with Brains before the silent aide left only to return minutes later with a handful of goons. Two of the largest carried a green, military metal case between them.

They dumped the chest down with a thud and after a nod from Merrick they opened it up.

"Yup, they're grenades all right," I said, stating the very obvious.

Another nod from the boss and the goons, plus grenades, left. "Now, what do I get out of this, Arthur?"

"You get a job done, by me. You know how good I am, and that's my offer."

"Deal."

"Okay, let's go," I said, this time really not wanting any more hold ups.

Merrick and Brains grabbed their jackets. Bespoke, three-quarter leather numbers that completed the sinister style. Black shirts, black jeans, black jackets, blacker hearts.

I was taken aback, this wasn't what I'd expected.

"What, you're both coming? I figured you'd just lend me the goons."

"And miss the chance to see a vampire? You've got to be fucking kidding."

So, off we went to blow up stuff, kill vampires, and stop them resurrecting the ashes of their long dead leader.

Just another day in the life of The Hat.

A Few Concerns

Merrick's goons took the lead in two cars, Vicky and I were next, and Brains drove Merrick in the last vehicle. I felt a little like the scruffy cousin nobody wants to talk to, jammed as I was between sparkling, top-of-the-range SUVs with tinted windows—proper gangster style.

One thing you could say about Merrick, he didn't hang about. Which was good, because we'd wasted enough time and I had to get inside the building before the vamps got all they'd ever dreamed of and more.

Now, you may be thinking, how come I was going for a full-frontal attack and was ready to blow up stuff when I'm meant to be a thief? Someone who sneaks about in the night? Good question. Honest answer?

Vampires were scary. Backup is always good, and what better backup than people who are hard as nails, have grenades, and you couldn't care less about? Exactly. Merrick was bad news through and through, and Brains was probably worse as he was a lot more calculating. Always whispering in Merrick's ear, weighing up decisions with his analytical mind. His lover, his companion, the smarts. The city would rest easier if they were dead, so it really was quite a good move on my part.

They either help and survive, which would be worth it, or they help and die, which would be ideal.

Only problem was Vicky, as I sure as hell didn't want anything happening to her.

"You killed that man, like it was nothing," were the first words she'd spoken for half an hour.

"I know. This isn't a game, it's a dangerous life, a dangerous business. You wanted in, this is what it's like." I was trying to be hard, tough love and all that, but it was difficult. I wanted to hold her hand, ask her if she was all right, but then what? She'd get over the death sooner, and want to continue.

"Bet you had a good reason, right? I know you, Arthur. You don't fool me."

"What do you mean?" I asked, giving her a steely glance, trying to remain a man of mystery.

"I mean, you're no cold-blooded killer. Sure, you get up to your japes, but—"

"Japes!"

"Your little hobby, stealing these artifacts and such, and I know you get into trouble and deal with the bad guys, but you aren't one yourself. So stop with the stupid squinting and spill it, mister, before I pinch your belly."

"You wouldn't dare," I said, giving up on my hard man look as it wasn't working.

The next thing I knew, Vicky was pinching me in the ribs and poking my belly button. I veered to the right then got control as Brains beeped his horn behind me and flashed his headlights.

"Behave. You'll get us into trouble," I warned.

"Spill it."

"Fine," I said, feeling deflated and wishing she wasn't so damn insightful. It's what came with being a mother, she could spot a lie a mile away. Damn Mom lie radar, how do they do it?

"The man I killed, Chaz, you heard him say I took something he was owed, something that was his. That I stole it from him?"

"I heard it. You made him slit his own throat, Arthur. What could be so bad? What did he do that was so awful you could do that to another person?"

"Vicky, I told you, this is a serious business. People have died today before Chaz, people always die. Why do you think I didn't want you here, sat beside me?"

"I'm a big girl," she said, folding her arms across her chest and squeezing her eyebrows together, "and if I spend one more night alone at the computer before dragging myself off to bed to hear the slug snore I'll top myself. I almost did it, you know, before."

"Shit, I'm sorry. You never said."

"Don't worry, I didn't go through with it."

"Oh, really?"

"Very funny. Okay, what did Chaz do?"

I took a deep breath, wishing I didn't have to dredge up old memories. The story would just have to be condensed, bare bones type of thing. "The item I took from him, that he was owed, was a sixteen-year-old girl. A man he had been bleeding dry, a guy running a business, trying to feed his family, couldn't pay, and Chaz was gonna make good on his threat. Merrick knew what he was like, but let it happen anyway. His utter contempt for others made Chaz one of the best enforcers out there. He always got paid as otherwise..."

"Oh my God, that's horrible. And Merrick knew he went around doing... Ugh, that he..."

"That he raped young girls, and boys, if their parents didn't pay? Yeah. I told you, these are not nice people. They disgust me, but there are worse than Merrick. It's why I got out of this kind of life and focused on the magic."

"Arthur, I never knew."

"Wish you'd cut his throat now?"

"Yes, I do." Vicky scratched at her neck without thinking, right where Merrick's scars were the worst. I had to hand it to her, she was one brave woman.

"So, stay out of their way. Leave them to blow open the gates and storm in acting all tough. If everything goes to plan, they'll be dead long before we get inside and then you leave the rest to me, okay?"

"Before we get inside?" Vicky wiggled her bum, enjoying the seat warmer and smiled at the thought of storming a vampire stronghold. What the hell was wrong with her?

"No, before I go inside. You wait in the car and you do not, under any circumstances, come into the house. Hell, Vicky, you gotta make the kids breakfast in what, four hours?"

"Plenty of time," she said as she tickled me again.

"Cut that out!"

What do they say about the best laid plans of mice and men? Ah, that's it. They never work out for men named Arthur.

Blood Moon

We'd arrive soon, and I got that calm feeling that always came over me as I shifted into the flow state. Peripheral nonsense faded as magic and mind melded, allowing me to function to the best of my ability.

Everything that could be in place was in place. Meaning, nothing at all was in place. The plan was fluid, typical Hat style. Some jobs needed meticulous planning and they always went wrong. The best, the smoothest ones, they were organic, unfolded along with events that, inevitably, became complicated and never went how I envisaged.

Merrick worked in a similar fashion, but with bells on. He relied on goons and fear, and I was keen to see how that'd play out against a real foe.

We were silent as we approached, the anticipation building, and I focused on the car in front, mesmerized by the lights.

Something distracted me, and I raised my eyes. No word of a lie, I almost slammed on the brakes and turned around and went right on home.

"Shit. Um, Vicky, you never mentioned anything about this in your damn internet search." I nodded out the front window.

"What? The car?"

"No, look up."

"Cool, that's so neat."

"Neat? Neat! It's a goddamn giant red moon. It looks like blood. Is this a special day? Is there gonna be an eclipse? The moon goes red during an eclipse doesn't it?"

"Nope, nothing like that. Just another full moon."

"Then why is it bright blood red?" This felt wrong, really wrong. Had this day been chosen especially? I'd never been big on superstition, as most things those involved in magic did was purely to get your head in the right space. To make you focus. If that meant performing a little dance out naked in the garden and chucking animal bones about, or chanting, or whatever, then it was understandable, but sometimes, just now and then mind you, cosmic events could, and did, influence what happened down on earth.

And a giant blood moon was, without doubt, not an omen I was particularly keen on. It may not mean anything in terms of magic, but if it held significance for the vampires it sure as hell would mean they had every intention of this working no matter what. To them, everything was perfectly aligned to resurrect the big boss man.

Vicky tapped away on her phone and I tapped away on the steering wheel. We were almost at the place I'd been taken to, minutes away, and I needed to know what else I was facing. The moon stared down at me, gloating. Calling me a fool and an impostor, taunting me. Telling me I was gonna die and so was Vicky. Our kids would be left alone in the world and it would all be my fault for being such an idiot and getting mixed up with Cerberus whether I knew about it or not.

"It's just a full moon," said Vicky, nonplussed. "Nothing special about tonight. There are harvest moons and hunter's moons and proper blood moons when there's an eclipse but none of that is today."

"So why the hell is it bright red?" I was getting panicky, flow state utterly gone. This was bad, I just knew it. Something was very wrong here and I was missing it.

"Hang on, hang on."

I tried to think when I'd seen a red moon before, and once I did I recalled that sometimes it was red as it rose low in the sky. Because of the sun having only just set, I always assumed. But the sun had set many hours ago, the moon was high overhead, and I'd never seen it looking like this.

"Ah, here we go." Vicky brushed her ponytail out the way and held up her phone to me.

"Just read it," I snapped. "I'm bloody driving here."

"Temper, temper, only trying to be helpful."

"Sorry, I'm used to insulting Pepper. He seemed to like it."

"Really?"

"Um, maybe. What does it say?"

"That sometimes the moon can appear red if there are particles in the sky. Blocks other colors or something like that."

Everything became clear as we rounded a bend and the house up high on the hill came into view. "Particles like ash?" I asked.

"Guess so." Vicky shrugged and put her phone away.

"Like ash from a huge fire that's right now burning down the house of the vampires? The vampires that are probably long gone, along with Mikalus' remains and our chance of stopping them?"

"Um, was that rhetorical?"

"I have no bloody clue."

I pulled up behind the goons and turned off the engine. We sat and watched the large vampire stronghold as it burned fiercely. The roof was almost consumed, tiles gone, rafters and half-incinerated batons stark and skeletal against the blood moon.

Then something gave way and the whole building collapsed in on itself with a mighty crash that made the car shudder.

"Come on, may as well take a look," I said with a sigh.

We got out the car. Gunfire tore through metal.

Drafted

There was a drawback to being a wildcat wizard. People tried to kill me. Sometimes they succeeded, which was why it helped to have a faery godmother. But Sasha was off bedding a mortal, so guess it was down to me.

"Duck!" I screamed, which sounded lame but was very pertinent.

"I'm already ducked," shouted Vicky from halfway under the car, retreating as she spoke until only her head was sticking out.

"Oh, good." I joined her quick smart.

"What's happening?" Vicky groped about in the dark, coffin-like space under the car and grabbed tight.

"Hey!"

"Oops, hehe. Sorry. Hey, firm butt. You been working out?"

"Actually, yes. I've been running, in the park. Ugh, what the hell is wrong with you? We're being shot at."

"And if I have to go, then I can't think of a better way then fondling your firm bottom."

Now wasn't the time, but it had to be said. "Look, Vicky, I really like you, but, er, as a friend. The 'accident' with the dressing gown earlier, and now this... I'm not sure how you got the wrong impression but—Ow!" I moved to put a hand to my backside where she'd slapped it but just knocked an elbow on the underside of the car.

"You idiot. That was an accident. And don't flatter yourself, mister. I don't think of you that way either." Vicky smiled her mom smile at me and, although it was utterly the wrong time to do so, we burst out laughing.

"Friends?"

"Friends forever."

"Which may not be for very long." I listened. The gunfire had stopped but a sound I was familiar with approached. "Damn."

"What?"

"I think we might be in a little trouble." I peered out at two ridiculously smart shoes attached to legs, one trailing the other slightly, aided by a cane. No guessing who it all belonged to.

The footsteps halted inches in front of our heads and with a slight grunt the man got down and peered under the car.

"Hello, Arthur."

"Oh, hello, Nathan. Nice to see you again. Pretty moon, isn't it?"

"Is this the guy who's arm you melted off?" asked Vicky, winning the prize for asking the most stupid question of the day

"Yes, my dear lady, I am he. Now, sorry to disturb your fondling, but would you mind awfully getting the fuck out from underneath the car? Please?"

"Only because you're asking so politely," I said, nodding to Vicky.

Magic at the ready, wand practically burning a hole in my pocket, I clambered out and Vicky did likewise.

Nathan smiled at us both. It wasn't a friendly smile.

I took in the wreck that was the car in front. It was riddled with holes. All four doors were open, every window was smashed, and four men lay very dead on the asphalt.

It was hard to see the lead car, but I assumed the goons had fared similarly. Behind us, Merrick's car was free of damage, the doors closed. Five heavily armed men stood guard with weapons aimed.

"Yours, I presume?"

"You can bet your life on it," said Nathan.

"I'd rather go home and have an early breakfast," which was no word of a lie.

"Sorry, Arthur, but you're drafted."

Ugh.

Any Objections

"Wait just one minute," I protested, magic almost leaking I was so close to using it.

"Arthur, if you so much as touch your wand, haha, then my men will destroy you. Both of you," said Nathan, voice more devoid of emotion than I'd remembered.

"Well, if you put it like that."

"I do."

"Now, shall we get to work?"

"I'd rather know what's going on first." I turned to look at the house. There was little left of it now. Even from such a distance I could taste the ash on my tongue, feel the warmth from such an ungodly bonfire.

The blood moon was still strong, a portent of a night far from done. A night alive with the sounds of sirens. Nathan seemed utterly unconcerned.

He glanced at his watch. "The local emergency services will arrive in a little under two minutes. You have a choice to make, Arthur, and you need to make it fast."

I put my hat back on my head and adjusted it at an angle, reconsidered, and tipped it forward a little. I remained silent.

"Tick tock, Arthur." Nathan spoke to Vicky. "Sorry, my dear lady, I didn't catch the name."

"Vicky, the name's Vicky."

"Well, Vicky, I do apologize for the inconvenience, but I'm guessing you are aware of today's events and are familiar with the rather unfortunate set of circumstances that see us standing here at this moment, waiting for Arthur to make up his mind about his, and your, future?"

"Yes."

"Good, just as long as we're on the same page." Nathan nodded as a large goon came up to him and whispered in his ear. Moments later the bodies were gone, the two lead cars too.

He seemed different to earlier, colder and less enamored with me for obvious reasons, but there was something else, too.

You know what? I'm such a muppet at times.

"Your arm!" I blurted.

"Later, if you're a good boy. Time's up, Arthur. The police and fire service will be here momentarily. Your choice. Oh, and what about them?" Nathan nodded and a belligerent Brains and Merrick were shoved hard in the back and prodded with very cool looking guns toward us.

"These, ah, gentleman, seem rather uncouth company to be keeping, Arthur. Not exactly the kind of fellows I would have expected you to use."

"Beggars can't be choosers," I replied, holding Merrick's gaze as he snarled at me, and everyone else.

"You're dead, Arthur. Her, too. And these spooks."

"Shut up, Merrick, you dick. You don't know who these guys are. You're out of your depth. Like way out."

"I advise quiet," said Brains, in a rare show of independence.

Nathan thought nothing of it, but for Merrick and I it was quite a shock. Brains never spoke to him like that. It just didn't happen. It was bad enough me standing up to him, but Brains, his man, nope.

"Time is up, what's it to be?"

"So dead. I'm gonna enjoy showing Vicky here, the little girl playing gangster, what real gangsters do to their enemies." Merrick licked his malformed lips with a fat, pink tongue.

"Kill 'em," I said.

It was over before Merrick could even register shock. A bullet to the head and he was down and definitely dead. Two spooks dragged him off and then it was Brains' turn. The gun raised, Vicky grabbed my hand and squeezed, Nathan nodded, and then everything was a blur.

A spook cried out, the sound cut off as he clutched his throat, then his head exploded as Brains snatched the man's gun and blew out his brains in one fluid motion. Not even slowing, he cracked the other spook over the nose and as he was blinded with pain Brains shot him right through his open mouth. The spinal column shattered as the bullet exited and the head lolled to a weird angle as he too dropped to the road.

As if he had all the time in the world, Brains turned and picked off the remaining men as they moved to take cover. He had the advantage as we acted like a shield, the spooks loathe to fire and risk hitting their boss.

We stood, shocked and silent, as Brains turned and said, "I think we need to re-evaluate the agreement you had with Merrick."

"I'm more than happy to do so," said Nathan, even though Brains was talking to me. Nathan kept his composure remarkably well when he was now at such a disadvantage.

"Good." Brains did the strangest thing then. He bent and kissed Merrick on the forehead, then stood and booted him hard in the body over and over until he was exhausted. Twenty kicks or more, sweat beading on his brow, breathing fast and hard, face full of hatred.

Whatever had gone on with those guys there was definitely something about the relationship that hadn't sat well with Brains, and that was the understatement of the year.

"Time to go," said Nathan. "This is far from ideal, Brains, is it? Look at the mess, but ho-hum, time for us to be on our way. Arthur, would you care to drive? My driver appears to have been shot in the face."

"Sure," I said, just wanting to get the hell out of there.

"I'll drive," said Brains.

Nobody argued.

Keepers

"In we get," said Nathan, nodding at my car.

"Where's yours?" I asked.

"My men have departed. We were to travel in your vehicles."

"I expected a Rolls, Nathan."

"This is business, Arthur, and the point is to be discreet. Not that we need worry about that anymore with the mess Brains here has made."

"You were ready to shoot me," said Brains, back to being emotionless as ever.

"Let's not quibble over the details. Now, if you would?" Nathan nodded forward at the road, flashing lights reflecting off the trees where the road curved. Already, the blood moon was fading as the fire was past its peak, returning to the cold, gray, silent eye I was more familiar with.

"Where to?"

"Just drive for now, I need to think."

Brains pulled off with practiced ease and we drove silently past a fleet of emergency services vehicles converging on the destroyed vampire compound.

"Sorry about Merrick," said Vicky. I gave her a nudge. "What?"

"Don't be sorry," said Brains. "That man was an animal."

Vicky and I exchanged a look and she remained silent. What a turn up for the books. I wondered what hold Merrick had had over Brains. It must have been something pretty damn nasty, but I got the feeling it was something he'd never talk about.

"This is all your fault, Nathan, you and your idiot brother," I said, unable to contain my anger at the absolute mess Cerberus had embroiled me in.

"Let's just say we are all to blame and leave it at that, shall we?"

"No, let's not. I get that Nigel went off the rails, was gonna hand the ashes over for whatever prize he felt justified his betrayal. But you, why in Buster's name didn't you tell me what I was holding? I would have gladly destroyed it."

Nathan said nothing and a thought came to me.

"Ah, so that's it. You guys don't want it destroyed, do you? You didn't tell me as you couldn't risk either me giving it to the vamps, or me getting rid of it, scattering it to the wind."

Nathan turned and said, "It's complicated."

"I'll bet. You went out on your own trying to get me, get the ashes, to protect your brother. Familial bonds and all that. But now I guess you have the Hounds behind you, and what, they still want it?"

"I received a thorough reprimand from my boss, but don't kid yourself, Arthur, I'm as high up in Cerberus as you will ever encounter. Everyone apart from one answers to me. I run this game, I make the decisions. Yes, we want Mikalus' ashes. Good God, man, it's too interesting and important a relic to destroy. Who knows what power it contains, when it may be needed? We must have it and we must ensure the vampires never use it."

"So you owned up, told your fellow Hounds what happened, and then what?"

"Then I got fixed up. We sent our people out to find you, which was ridiculously easy. You really should be more careful. Then we waited for you to lead us to the vampires."

"I'd have thought you guys would already know where the vampires were based, what with you being so damn smart."

"Arthur, you really have no idea, do you?"

"Enlighten me."

"You wizards, you're all the same. You never take the time to learn about what's actually going on."

"Wrong, Nathan. What I'm beginning to think is that Cerberus makes it its duty to ensure we don't know what's going on. You like to be the ones with the most information, so do whatever it takes to keep us in the dark."

"Haha, there are things best not known by the common wizard. Okay, history lesson time. There are many thousands of these sub-vampires. They have homes, families, some live communally like in the building we watched burn, others alone. Some in bedsits, others in mansions, and we track as many as we possibly can. But there are worse things than these pathetic creatures. Many of them are Twenties, Thirties, Forties, or even weaker. Their power is so negligible, their abilities so subtle, that you'd hardly even know what they were. You and your wizard brothers have been too complacent for too long, and whatever you may think of us, that isn't our fault. You don't look because the vampires don't cause much trouble, but it doesn't mean they won't. It's left to us to keep everyone safe. The magical community has no idea what goes on right under their noses."

"I know more than enough, thank you very much. I know about the weakness of the newer vamps. Sure, I didn't know how many there were, but as you say, there are plenty more pressing things to worry about."

"True. But now there isn't."

"Back at the park, that dude could have killed you, but he didn't. Why?"

"Because they are not the creatures most believe them to be. They are like us in many regards. Some are nice, some not so nice. But it changes nothing."

"Okay, I get it. Fair enough. But why not destroy the ashes? It makes no sense."

"Because it's so powerful. Cerberus protects humanity from its own idiocy, from abusing magic. But we still respect the supernatural and have made an oath to preserve, not destroy."

"You've got a funny way of showing it," I said.

"That's the most stupid thing I've ever heard," said Vicky who'd been listening intently and had somehow managed to so far remain silent.

Brains acted like we were talking about the weather. I caught a glimpse of him in the rearview. His face was utterly impassive, but he would be soaking up this information and planning how to use it to his advantage. Whatever had gone on between him and Merrick, one thing remained certain. He was bad news and we'd pay for what had happened, regardless.

"Cerberus has been powerful for thousands of years. We protect the world from dangerous artifacts. We keep them safe, we help."

"Spare me that bullshit," I spat, anger rising. "You're a bunch of do-gooders who take what isn't yours and keep it for yourselves. Cerberus doesn't care about magic users, you've got an agenda and you know it. What about people? You don't help them. You just want the relics, the books, the things. You're a bunch of religious zealots and sneaky as fuck. Protecting us from ourselves? Bollocks. I don't buy it and neither do other wizards. You guys don't even learn magic yourselves, you just take magical items and probably arrange them nicely in some lovely display room somewhere and beat off to them like the bunch of wackos you are."

Nathan turned again and I could see my words had made a real impact. He was beyond angry, he was affronted and insulted. "You don't know what you're talking about," he snapped. "You have absolutely no idea. Our order has meaning, is more important than you can imagine. I am a Hound, and same as all fellow Hounds, those tasked with important work, we know magic. You are mistaken about us. So very mistaken. You would do well to watch your tongue, Arthur."

"Or what?"

"Or I'll ensure you never see another sunrise. Do I make myself clear? Do I?"

"Whatever."

"Turn off here if you would be so kind, Brains," asked Nathan, back to being the upper-class, emotionless twat that he undoubtedly was.

Brains parked and Nathan pulled out a phone, tapped away, sent a text message and then the car was silent.

"What now?" I asked.

"Now? Now we wait. And then, when I'm ready, we go get Mikalus' ashes from wherever the vampires have taken them. Tell me Arthur, who was in the house? Who did you deal with? Was it a Fourth? Why did they let you leave alive?"

I smothered a smile. For all his big talk about knowing what was happening in the world, it was all a front. They didn't know everything. If they believed Fourths were the highest up still around then let them believe that. I wasn't about to share what I knew with him, with them.

"Guess so, he seemed pretty powerful. As to letting me live, they stick to their word, Nathan. There was a deal, the original deal that was made when I agreed to do the job. What I asked Nigel for. He obviously told them what I wanted and they agreed, and delivered. They stuck to their word, understand?"

"I do. They place great merit in being people, ex-people, of honor, hold it sacred. And what recompense did you receive?"

I resisted the urge to pat my pocket where the package was, knowing this was another thing best kept to myself. "Oh, you know, the usual."

"I see."

Nathan seemed satisfied with that. He'd assume it was money in a bank account somewhere. Let him believe that. The less he knew, the better.

His phone buzzed and he checked his message.

"Ah, our people have found the most likely location. Not confirmed, but it will be within minutes. Brains, are you sure you are happy to drive? And I know this must be confusing for you, I apologize. You're remarkably silent for someone who has heard so much outlandish conversation, are you not surprised?"

"Nothing surprises me. I've seen enough to convince me what you all say is true. And Merrick may not have believed Arthur is a real wizard, but I knew. Where to?"

"One moment, please." Nathan kept an eye on his phone, checked the new message when it came, and nodded in satisfaction. He gave directions and off we went.

I had no doubt that Nathan would try to kill us all at the first opportunity. If they had found the vampires with the ashes then we were now nothing but a liability.

The longer we drove back toward the city, and the more directions Nathan gave, the more uncomfortable I became. I couldn't sit still. The seatbelt felt too tight, the seat too lumpy. I was too hot, too cold, didn't have enough room. Vicky was breathing, which was annoying, and Nathan kept tapping his cane. And what was that all about? Dude had his arm fixed, no doubt by using his cane, maybe his own magic, or something Cerberus had, and yet he still had a limp.

"What's the matter with you? Keep still," moaned Vicky as I wriggled about.

"Sorry, but I've got a bad feeling about this."

"We'll be fine."

"No, we won't. But that's not it. I think I know where we're going."

"Figured it out, have you?" asked Nathan without turning.

"I hope not," I said, knowing I deserved a smack about the head for being complacent.

As if reading my thoughts, Nathan said, "Yes, they must have followed you, Arthur. Very careless of you."

I racked my brain, trying to think back on the day and how the hell the vampires could have worked it out. I came up with nothing. It could have been at any time. Somehow, they knew I was to be the one to get the ashes for them and had gone out of their way to follow me, maybe to snatch the ashes if I failed. Or, and thinking back on it this seemed more likely, so they could allow me to walk out of there after the handover, keeping to their sacred word, as they knew they could reach me if they needed to.

"Here we are," said Nathan just a few minutes later. "If you could pull up as close to number seven as possible please, Brains. Lucky for some, eh, Arthur?" said Nathan with a smile that didn't touch his eyes.

"Fuck off."

"Now, now, that's no way to talk to someone who has brought you home."

"Home?" asked Vicky. "I thought you lived on a farm, not in a small terraced house?"

"I do," I said with a sigh. "This is just the front door."

A Violation

"I don't understand," said Vicky, chewing on the corner of her lip, both nervous and annoyed, thinking I'd lied to her.

"This is why Arthur's no easy man to track down. I have to hand it to you, Arthur, you had us fooled."

I just glared at Nathan, his fair hair a sickly yellow under the glow of the streetlight one house down from what really was just my front door.

"Arthur?" Vicky went from lip biting to lip trembling. I knew I had to talk and talk fast before the tears began. Hell, what use was a sidekick if she'd get all weepy if she thought I'd been keeping a few secrets? I was a bloody wildcat wizard, of course there were secrets.

"Well, tell her. Actually, before we go any further, I'd like an explanation, too."

I took a few deep breaths, tried not to think about what was happening outside my home, as there were sure to be numerous overexcited vampires running loose, and tried to put the pieces together before I spoke.

Nathan, and probably Nigel, must have known where I lived. There was no other explanation for the amateur that had threatened me on the road to my house earlier that day. He would have been fairly local to have made it there with little warning, and was the first person from the underground to have found me. That was how. Nathan had known where I was.

But the vampires, how did they know? Nigel. He must have betrayed me, told them so they'd trust him, offer him what he wanted.

Ugh, what a ridiculous mess. Life was never normally this complicated. Yes, I got into a few scrapes and sometimes things went rather wonky, but this day was worse than almost any I could remember. Even as I thought such thoughts, I recalled several terrible jobs and the aftermath, and I gotta say, it made me feel a little better. There were, rather surprisingly, a multitude of incidents much worse, but I guess I'm a glass half full kinda guy and had put them to the back of my mind.

"Arthur, stop daydreaming," said Vicky, nudging me.

"Sorry. Okay, very quick then we have to go. This is bad, right, Nathan?"

"Oh, you can bet on it. We have people going the long way around as I assume you have certain safeguards in place that cannot be disabled."

"Of course I do, I'm not a complete amateur." What a bloody cheek! Who did he think he was dealing with? Don't answer that, you're not seeing me at my finest.

"As you say. Please, continue, but be quick. They are there, Arthur, and you aren't going to like it."

"I bet I won't. Okay, look, Vicky, I don't live here, I live miles away, in Cornwall. By the coast in a tiny village called Mousehole. It's quiet, and it's safe. I'm out a mile from the village, and I really do live on a farm."

"But this is a two up two down in one of the worst parts of the city," protested Vicky.

"You'll see," I said, wishing nobody had to.

"This I have got to see," said Nathan. "There's only one way for this to be possible, and Cerberus have been looking for it for millennia. How'd you do it, Arthur? How'd you get it, find it?"

"Because I'm good at what I do," I replied testily. Honestly, I usually was.

"I know that. We would never have been using you all these years unless you were about the best there was."

Nathan wasn't paying me a compliment, he was stating fact. Not that being used like this made me feel better, but it was nice to get recognition. Yeah, The Hat had some real mad skills.

"Okay, let's go kill lots of vampires," I said with a sigh.

All I could think about was George. It was the middle of the night. Should I call her, just to be safe? No, why worry her? Then I whispered, "Screw it," and fished out my phone, smiling as my fingers brushed past the package still in my pocket.

I called. It rang and rang but she didn't pick up.

It didn't mean anything. She was just a heavy sleeper and often didn't hear the phone when I'd called in the night then rushed home in a panic only to find her safe and sound, sleeping so deeply a nuclear explosion wouldn't wake her.

She was fine, nothing to worry about.

I was worried as hell.

A Homecoming

As we got out the car, I forced myself to focus, to calm my beating heart. George would be okay. There was no reason for the vampires to go to my house, and they couldn't get in even if they'd wanted to.

I kicked myself in the ankle, hard, because I deserved it. Yes, they could. If they'd broken the wards on my front door here, they could get inside my house there. But why bother at all? Safety? Just to get away from Cerberus, make their life more difficult? It didn't make sense. I was missing something, but then a thought came to me.

There was something they needed, something they couldn't get here. There was no reason to burn down their house unless to eradicate any evidence of themselves, start afresh, or destroy something they no longer needed. However hard I tried, I could think of no logical reason for them to go to this amount of trouble to get away.

Were they after me? Was that why they'd vanished through my front door? No, as if they were this good they'd know where I was, and I believed they were that good.

What then?

My heart sank. More. It fell to the floor and got stomped on. Not wanting to believe it, I turned to Vicky.

"Listen, this is important. I mean the most important thing in the world."

"Okay," she said warily. "What is it? You're scaring me, Arthur."

"You finally figured it out?" said Nathan. "Why do you think I wanted to hurry?"

"Shut your fucking mouth! What is with you? Why don't you just tell me, rather than playing these idiotic games?"

"Because I'm in charge, Arthur, not you. This happens how I say, you do what I say. Understand?"

"Just shut up." I turned back to Vicky. "What did that professor say about the ritual? How they got it to work?"

"Something about a score of Children of the Blood, one for each century, no more, no less. That stuff about the circle and all the other rituals. The bathing, the cleansing, and everything. What? What is it?"

"Wait a minute, I'm trying to think." I hadn't paid enough attention when Vicky had read the stuff about the ritual to resurrect Mikalus, more concerned with how long it would take them to do it than anything else. The cleansing. The final cleansing before the ritual proper began. Before they resurrected Mikalus.

What had Vicky said?

"Ugh, I can't remember. What did they say about the cleansing? How they actually resurrected him?" I asked, almost shaking her in my panic.

"Something about pure ones. Being unsullied," said Vicky, looking at me with something close to fear in her eyes. Fear of me.

"And you shall be cleansed by the pure one, unsullied and touched by the universe," said Nathan.

"They mean a virgin witch, don't they? That's what the words mean?" I knew it was right, but wanted to hear Nathan say it.

"Yes. They each have to take her blood, be cleansed by a witch who has, er, never known a man."

Half of me felt pleased that George had a boyfriend, and she was seventeen, and all girls that age had sex nowadays didn't they? Or so I'd heard. For once I really regretted not having "that" conversation with her, just so I could be sure. But teenagers lie anyway, don't they? She would have probably told me to shut up and said it was none of my business.

Or had she not slept with her boyfriend? Was she still pure? What a ridiculous way to put it. Pure. Unsullied. As if such a beautiful thing as sex made you dirty somehow. Guess the morals and attitudes of ancient vampires were different to the modern ones, although maybe not.

A witch was a rare thing compared to wizards. Don't ask me why. It's just the way it was. Sure, there were plenty, but I guess it had always been a bit of a boys' club. And virgin witches? You could count them on one hand as it took years of training and most couldn't even perform the simplest of magic until well into their twenties or thirties, often later. That went for men and women both. Maybe my daughter was the only virgin witch in the country. Maybe that's why they wanted me to get the ashes for them, because they knew all about me. Knew who I was and about my daughter, and wanted not only the ashes but to find out where George was as they needed her if this was to happen any time soon.

"Let's go. We are definitely going to spill blood this night."

I walked to the door and knew in an instant the wards had been tampered with. They were back, to a degree, but were off slightly. They'd surprised the vampires with the backups I had in place, and I knew there'd be a few bodies, but the rest had got through. These guys had some serious magic of their own.

"What, we all going?" I asked, turning to everyone crowded around me. I was answered with mute nods. "Fine. Here goes nothing."

I took off my hat, removed the small circular charm on the short silver chain pinned to it, and placed it over what looked like a keyhole but was for a unique kind of key. As the circle, with a personal and intricate shape inside touched the magic-infused silver of the recess, it sparkled faintly with an ethereal glow and the lock likewise. The wards drifted away from the door like idle thoughts and with a creak I'd put in place just because all mysterious doors should creak, the door badly in need of a paint-job eased open to reveal an ordinary hallway with a cheap carpet and a basic kitchen on view at the rear of the tiny house.

Plus two small piles of ash where the first to enter had tripped the backups.

"It's just a house," said Brains, looking curiously inside.

"I thought you said it was—"

"Just hold hands and walk," I said, interrupting Vicky.

With Brains first, then Nathan, then Vicky, and me bringing up the rear, we held hands and walked forward along the narrow, dim hall, lit only by a bulb I left on at all times, covered with a paper lantern thick with dust. I closed the door behind us, quickly put the wards back in place, although it felt rather futile, attached the charm to my hat, and said, "Just keep walking. You have to go under the arch."

Everyone stared from me to the rather oversized archway with two supporting pillars that blended roughly with the walls. It was plain, hardly worth a second glance. I'd plastered over it myself just in case of prying eyes, but beneath the plaster and the magnolia paint resided one of the most spectacular, amazing, downright incredible magical items in the history of humanity.

The Gates of Bakaudif. One here, its twin at the other end. Remind me to tell you how I got them some time, it's quite a story.

"Go, just go," I sighed.

Brains, only pausing for a second, shrugged his shoulders and walked. Vicky gasped as first he then

Nathan disappeared and she turned to me, afraid. "Don't let go," I warned, "and keep walking."

She nodded, faced front, and I followed her through as she vanished.

My daughter better not be a virgin, was probably the strangest thought any father had ever had about his child. But right now I wished with all my heart that she'd got it on with at least somebody.

As long as he never set foot in my house because then I'd kill him. That's what fathers do, right?

No Car

"Bugger, they stole my car." I wasn't surprised, but it was damn inconvenient. "What, why are you all looking at me funny?"

"That was, without doubt, the most amazing thing I have ever experienced," said Nathan, face lit up like the vampires' old house.

"Awesome," said Brains, turning and peering at the narrow arched entrance we'd emerged through. It looked like a simple archway into a tiny room from the main part of the barn, but behind the rough plasterwork it housed the other of the only two Gates of Bakaudif still in existence.

"We just teleported!" Vicky clapped her hands together in glee and did a little jig. "Wait until I tell the kids."

I knew this was a bad idea. "Vicky, you can't tell the kids. You can't tell anyone, ever. Brains, I wouldn't dream of telling you what to do, but you cannot talk of this, understand?" I tried to be polite, but he still scowled and went rigid at my words.

"I won't, but not because you told me not to," he said, sounding like a petulant child.

"Whatever. Now's not the time to play gangster."

"I'm not a gangster, I'm a victim. Now I'm free and—"

"Bullshit, don't give me that. You and I both know that if you get out of this alive you're going to go run Merrick's business, like you already do. Spare me the excuses."

"As you wish." Brains wandered away down the straw-laden floor of the cavernous barn.

I bought the plot of land it stood on, and the barn, for a ridiculous price years before, part of my move to a safer place. It was very impressive. Huge vaulted roof, everything built without a single nail. Just expert carpentry and the sides filled in with brick, flint, anything the original builders could lay their hands on. It had stood for centuries and wasn't going anywhere any time soon.

Perfect for storing cars—I changed them constantly, both here and in the city, often forgetting what I owned or which one I was currently driving— and sundry items I might need when going to the city. But no car, and that was bad.

"We're like the first people to travel through a portal," marveled Vicky, looking so tiny and frail in the huge space.

I wished I hadn't got her involved, had thought she'd bail, but she really was loving this. But there was no time to think about that now, we had to get moving.

"Nathan, you got people coming to get the vampires, right?"

"Yes, but they'll be a while. We could have brought people with us but time is more important than number of bodies so let's get to this."

His veneer was cracking, the clipped tones getting sloppy, the words more relaxed. I wondered if he was anything like the person he presented, or someone else entirely.

"We're a couple miles from my house, so even if someone came through they still wouldn't know where to go. It's a long walk, so it'll be best to cut across down to the village, get a car, and drive. It'll be quicker."

"Let's go!" shouted Vicky, and marched through the barn, ponytail bouncing. Didn't this woman understand the trouble we were in?

With fear mounting, a sense of urgency overriding my ability to think logically and come up with a plan, all I could think of was get a car, drive home, and make sure George was safe.

I hurried to catch up with the others, all now waiting at the barn door.

"Wait!" I shouted, but it was too late. Vicky lifted the large latch, pulled on the door, then flew thirty feet backward as a dark shape darted out.

Then another, and another.

A Hold-Up

I ran back to Vicky while she was still bouncing along the floor, rolled up tight in a ball, head tucked in. Finally, she came to a stop and I got to her a moment later and said, "Damn, you've done this before."

"It's all the gymnastics as a kid, plus I practice with the girls." She smiled and sprang to her feet, seemingly none the worse for being thrown like a rag doll.

"That's my girl. Stay back here, but don't," I warned, "go back through the portal without me. You'll be fried to a crisp, understand?"

"Aye, aye, my captain."

I turned and ran back toward the three men blocking the doorway. The barn doors were wide open now, revealing a full moon high above the sea in the distance. Ghoulish moonlight reflected on the water like tiny spectral ships. There was the faintest hint of light pollution below the rise of the hill where the tiny village of Mousehole slept peacefully, unawares a battle for not only their future but that of humanity was ready to be raged above.

Oh, how I longed for this to be one of the days when I wandered through the village, breathing deep of salt-heavy air tinged with the tang of vinegar as tourists flocked to the fish and chip shop in their droves and batted at seagulls as they dove to pinch the steaming morsels right out their hands.

"You better not have touched her," I warned the three men blocking our way.

"She will be safe if you allow us to finish our work," said a man to the right. I turned my attention to him but it was hard to keep him in focus, so ordinary was he, so entirely forgettable. This was no Tenth or Twentieth or however far along they were now, this was maybe a Third, Fourth at most. The more removed from Mikalus, the more like real people they were, and this guy was far from real people, same as the other two.

Guess they'd drawn the short straw and been put on guard duty, but if all went well they'd still get their chance. Become true Seconds with all the power that entailed. Although, it was a little hazy as to what that might truly be.

"No way will I let you touch a hair on her head. She's my daughter."

"As I said, she will be protected. She will be safe. She will be free."

I didn't like the way he said free. Free as in free to go? Or free as in, "Look, I'm a vampire, and free of fear of death?"

"You mean you'll turn her?"

"She is the chosen one," was all he said. Cryptic bugger. I'd show him cryptic.

That did it, I reached for my wand but felt powerful resistance around my wrist as I did so. Brains held fast and, eyes doing a strange flickering thing, changing shape, blinking fast, said, "I will deal with these creatures and I will catch you up. You owe me, Arthur, 'The Hat' Salzman. I expect something in return."

I nodded, and watched as he carefully removed first his watch, placing it aside, then proceeded to strip.

Everyone was silent, mesmerized by the calm actions of a tall and skinny man with a very serious, almost plastic expression as he took off his clothes without any hint of embarrassment or concern.

Vicky gasped and put a hand to her mouth as his smart black shirt was removed, revealing a terrible corruption of scars across both his back and front. Brains was a mess, livid tracks of viciousness splashed across ghostly flesh. An abstract painting come to life. The marks were no result of knife fights or any kind of weapon. No, these were from entirely natural weapons. Teeth and claws. Over many years, he'd been slashed, gouged, chewed on and worse. His left pectoral was grisly, terribly malformed with a chunk off the side. A wild, raw, pink confusion of scar upon scar where flesh had knitted back badly.

Naked, Brains said, "So it begins," and stepped forward.

The vampires spread out. Nathan moved aside, and so did Vicky and I, leaving Brains in the center of the barn, naked but for his black cotton socks. I was about to tell him, but figured it would spoil the moment, so remained silent as he lifted his head, turned to me, and said, "You're lucky this happened today."

Brains lifted his chin, closed his eyes as if in ecstasy, and the tight skin on his neck bulged as his Adam's apple grew and poked hard as if ready to burst through. A guttural rumble emanated from his stretched mouth, lips pared back to reveal teeth like ivory. Then he howled at the full moon, a primeval sound that made adrenaline surge and the hairs on my arms stand on end.

With a throaty scream like he was giving birth to a fifty pound baby, he fell to his hands and knees. His entire body spasmed then vibrated so fast he was nothing but a blur of white flesh then brown.

In a matter of seconds the change was complete.

The lycanthrope pounced.

A Rare Insight

The therianthropic creature was mostly wolf, but not quite. Although, to be fair, it was rather dark and Brains, or what was Brains, moved damn fast. Wolf-man, man-wolf, half-and-half, or whatever he was.

Old vampires were fast, and mightily strong, and these Fourths were good for their number, but one thing they were not, was man-wolves with the teeth and claws to go with it.

Brains made short work of them. It was horrifying to watch, but watch I did. These men threatened my daughter and I'd see them stripped of their flesh and faces. They deserved it, and worse.

The creature tore through the last vampire's belly with a sickening squelch. Vicky buried her face in my chest as the innards were snapped at with red and brown stained teeth. The huge, malformed jaw of the creature flung organs and muscle into the shadowy recesses, food for the rats and mice, then lifted its head, shook once, before tearing out the throat in one swift movement as he had the others. The vampire died.

Good riddance. Not because of what they were, we all had our faults, but because of what they'd threatened.

Vicky kept peeking from where she'd buried her head, disgusted yet drawn to the horrifying display of unbridled animal violence. I understood, had done it myself, seen it happen on many occasions. There was something perversely compelling about witnessing acts of violence. You felt sick to your stomach, wanted to heave and hide and run away, and your body shakes and your mind reels at the sights you ought never to see, yet you have to look. Like watching a horror movie when you know it will be scary but you look anyway, peeking between your fingers.

It's the utter uniqueness of the situation. For Vicky, she was witnessing something she had never seen before in her life. True violence. The squishy bits of a person meant to remain inside, never to be gazed upon. The blood and crunched bone, the half-digested food and the waste products leaking and oozing and squirting between fangs, she was almost compelled to look because of its utter strangeness and surreal horror.

Then it was over, and Brains withdrew from the vampires, making strange mewling sounds like an injured dog. Whimpering and snuffling, body trembling uncontrollably. He was no unthinking animal, there was a strong sense of self inside the body of the half-wolf. Brains was very unusual. Shifters could control their change, but when they did it they were the animal. Most could shift at any time but Brains was different. He was tied to the moon. Could become the wolf but maintain a semblance of the man. Meaning, he was much more dangerous than those that shifted into an animal, for he could plan, think, second-guess his opponent and use his considerable intellect to outwit and destroy them.

The obvious drawback being he was limited to maybe a few days each month, but what he lacked in ability to change at will he sure as hell made up for in ferocity.

How in Buster's name had Merrick kept this guy on a leash for so many years? He was smart, could do this, and clearly wasn't afraid to use violence. No way should Merrick have survived as long as he had, let alone make Brains do his bidding. Guess I'd find out, if he lived. If any of us lived.

"You okay?" I whispered into Vicky's ear.

She lifted her head and said, "No, not really. He just... just tore them apart. I didn't think things like this could happen."

"They can happen. And worse. He's a rare kind of man, turns into the wolf but remains a man, too. He helped us, but it wasn't pretty." I didn't know what else to say. There was no point chastising her for wanting to tag along, she already knew it would be dangerous, but there's a difference between romanticizing an adventure and being in the middle of it and realizing it's a lot more scary and a lot more visceral than you could have imagined.

I hoped this would make her see sense and go home to her kids. But I also knew Vicky and above all else she was stubborn. She'd see this through to the bitter end no matter what. I had to make the offer, though.

"You want me to take you back? It will only take a minute and you can be home. Go to bed and pretend like this never happened."

Vicky pushed away from me, took in the sight of the mangled corpses and Brains hunched over half in shadow, body already cracking and morphing back into that of a tall, skinny man. "No, we have to get George, and I'm just as much a part of this as you are now. I'm involved and I won't ever sleep again unless I know this is over with."

"Okay, I understand."

Maybe this was the true reason why I could never sleep. I said nothing, but what Vicky was about to learn was that it was never over. There were always things lurking in the shadows in the world I walked in and she'd chosen to step over the line and join me. There was no going back. Ever.

There was no peace, there was no rest, there was always something bad ready to rip away your sanity.

Makes you wonder why I trod this path, doesn't it? But maybe I was just like Cerberus, a Hound without the name. My own personal crusade to ensure the wonders of this world belonged to the right people, or at least didn't get to stay with the wrong ones.

Or, and I regret to say I think this is probably the real truth, I liked this wildness, the buzz, the sense of danger and ability to take the moral high ground.

I was a soldier without a country to fight for. Once you've been a part of the wilder, more dangerous side of life, the mundane world with its petty concerns seems ridiculous, unimportant, and bland. You want to stand in the middle of the street and shout, "Don't you know what's happening? I've killed and I've been killed. I've lived, I've felt the rush. I've wielded mighty forces and I have taken charge of my life and chosen to walk on the side of the angels and demons. What have you done?"

But, just like soldiers once they are no longer fighting a war, I didn't. When around regular folk I kept quiet, acted as normal as I could, but I saw it in those who'd witnessed the truth of this world. The edginess in their eyes, the sense of something missing they had, the emptiness inside.

And given half the chance I'd jump right back into the madness just to feel alive.

Mousehole

Brains dressed calmly and without looking at us, taking the time to clean himself with wet wipes that seemed rather convenient to have unless he'd been expecting to change. There was no point saying anything, certainly no point forging on ahead without him. We were all in this together and he was an asset, if a rather worrying one.

Soon enough, he was dressed and came to join us, acting as though nothing had happened.

"Let's go," I said. "And thanks."

"Like I said, you owe me." Brains adjusted his shirt collar, checked himself over, and then did a strange thing. He frowned at his tie, then undid it and yanked it from his neck. "Always hated wearing a tie." He stomped on it then walked out the barn.

Nathan remained stoic as always, just turned up his nose at the smell and the mess, taking it all in his stride.

"This is all your fault. What is wrong with you?" I said quietly to him as we made our way across the fields toward Mousehole.

"As I told you, we didn't know if we could trust you, so had to try to get the ashes by other means."

"You put my daughter's life in danger, you put everyone's life in danger. Just so you can be the hero, the one that made sure Cerberus got their prize. You could have stopped this, you could have warned me, told me, and you could have had it."

Nathan moved fast to keep pace with me, but it obviously cost him. "Arthur, don't play games with me. If I'd told you who I was, who we really were, then what, you'd have just handed over the ashes and that would have been that?" I remained silent. "Exactly. You may not have given the bag to the vampires but you wouldn't have given it to me either. And it would have made no difference. We would have still been after you and the vampires, too. I did you a favor."

"Some favor. You put George at risk."

"No, you did that. You took something, agreed to a job without knowing what it meant. That's on your shoulders, my friend, don't try to put the blame on me. I know what I'm involved in, you too, and you know the risks."

I sped up to catch Vicky. He had a point, but I'd trusted Nigel, never thought he'd cross me like this. He'd betrayed me, just like Pepper had, and they were both dead.

We forged ahead, moving fast, nobody talking. Before long we were above the village, brightly painted houses palely reflecting the light of the moon, huddled close together as if for warmth through the night. As we entered the village, it was as if it knew this was no regular night, that strange things were afoot. Houses seemed to lean across the narrow streets to warn their neighbors. Be quiet, go to sleep. There are strange creatures in the village and they mean us harm.

The place was deserted, not a soul in sight. Just a few cats that ran for cover as we approached, watching with wide eyes from behind pots of plants that would be bright in the daylight, there to cheer up the fronts of houses that opened right onto the cobbled streets.

We made it down to the harbor where fishing and recreation boats bobbed languidly on the water. Everything still, everything quiet, everything feeling wrong. My village, my home, had been violated. I kept my work well away from here, lived a peaceful and quiet life, chatting with the shop owners, nodding at the fishermen when I sat by the harbor early in the mornings, sleep eluding me.

I liked it here. It was so far removed from the craziness of the cities, from the dark places I went with dark intentions and where death was always ready to pounce. Here it was a different life. Everyone smiled, and chatted to their neighbors, where the pace of life was slow and there were no gangsters, no monsters, no thieving and no murder. Crime was next to non-existent, the tourists brought in money, and the winters were wondrous.

The number of houses owned by those only using them on weekends or a few times a year was a major bone of contention but there was nothing to be done about it. Out of season, the village was almost deserted, the streets quiet, only the locals out and about. It had a different feel then, one I enjoyed. A true sense of living in the past, everything simpler. Even now, walking the streets, I got that sense of otherworldly innocence, and I'd walked through the village no end of times, summer and winter, finding this sense of peace.

There was room to breathe, to think, to take in the scent of fish and salt and feel the wind on my face. Well away from the beeping of car horns and the constant shouting and chaos of the city.

This was my home, my true home, and I'd brought death and malice to its doorstep.

Time to clean up the mess and make sure it never came back.

Arthur was ready to take out the trash.

A Drive Home

My nerves felt frayed as I touched my wand to the door of a rather swanky BMW and it sprang open. Wasting no time, we piled in and I again let a trace of magic channel through me, out the wand, and the car started. It wasn't a local's, so I didn't feel quite as bad, and all things being well, it would be back before the owners woke in the morning.

Yeah, exactly. Not a hope in hell of them ever seeing it again.

I headed home, having to control my speed as the tight turns and narrow lanes meant an accident was likely unless I got a grip.

"How long before your people get here?" I asked Nathan.

"We had a few less than an hour away so they should be arriving right about now. But the main group are some way out, they'll be a good hour, maybe more."

"So no use at all. Guess it's just us and a couple of your spooks then, if they make it."

"Guess so." Nathan didn't seem unduly worried, and that made me worry more. All he cared about were the ashes and owning them for his nutty friends. Not my daughter, not me. Not Vicky. Brains could take care of himself, but George was just a kid, and Vicky was a mother.

The last stretch of road was a straight run so I put my foot down and tried not to freak out. My heart was hammering so hard in my chest I worried about a stroke, but I was unable to calm myself, couldn't stop my mind conjuring up images of George surrounded by vampires with the ashes of Mikalus at the center. Each vampire taking a bite of her, chanting, and lost to desire. Then it was done, and Mikalus rose from the ashes, a terrible Phoenix reborn. Powerful, invincible, the original vampire.

Hungry.

I saw George, eyes wide and frightened, shouting and screaming as the terrible body of Mikalus unfolded, revealing his true self, before he shrouded her in his tattered arms and bent her back, exposing her neck, then bit and drank deeply, her legs kicking as he drained her.

Then she was dying on the floor, and the last thing she saw of this world was the man who killed her and I was nowhere to be seen. I'd abandoned her to the monsters.

I mumbled, "No," and drove faster.

There was no way I'd let that happen. She would not die, she would not be taken from me. I shook my head to clear the fog, began to draw power, focusing every ounce of my being on the magic. Willing it to consume me, to give me the strength I needed to tear through the vampires, obliterate them and save my child.

We were there. I slammed my foot on the brake and skidded to a halt at the gate.

"Where is everyone?" asked Vicky, unbuckling her seatbelt and leaning forward between the seats.

"That's a very good question," I said.

The place looked the same as always. The exterior lights highlighted the cobbled courtyard, the barns, the mud, the house. Everything was quiet, everything as it should be. No sign of anyone or anything untoward.

My heart sank.

Intruder Alert

"Everyone out," I ordered.

"You don't get to be in charge," said Nathan.

"I'll tell you what, Nathan. When it's your daughter being eaten by vampires then you can have your turn, okay? Until then, shut the fuck up and get out of the fucking car or I swear to God I will make more than your arm melt. Do you hear me?"

For a moment he hesitated, and I wondered what he thought he could do. But then he sighed as if to mollify a petulant child and said, "As you wish. But if you interfere with our plans, you will never see the sun rise. Do I make myself clear?"

"Just get out," I whispered, no strength left for such games.

Nathan and Brains got out the car and I moved to exit. "Wait," said Vicky, putting a hand to my arm.

"What is it? I'm kinda busy here." Vicky held my gaze and I lowered mine. "Sorry, I'm stressed. Didn't mean to snap."

"Arthur, it's okay. Look, just remember one thing."

"Okay. What?"

"You're The Hat and nobody fucks with you." She smiled, and then she set her jaw in determination, the look she got that told the world she would have her own way, no matter what.

I nodded, and smiled back at her. "I'm The Hat, nobody fucks with me."

"Better?"

"Better," I agreed, and we got out of the car.

Standing in the mud outside the gate, I paused to listen but heard nothing. From here the house looked the same as always, just a hint of light from between the curtains that could have meant anything or nothing. George wasn't exactly an eco warrior and seemed to have an uncanny knack for turning on, and leaving on, all lights she had no intention of using for at least twelve hours. Something they did to all teenagers at a secret teenager lab designed to make parents question if they had any form of long-term memory whatsoever.

The exterior lights didn't reach this far from the house and we were in almost complete darkness. So, with sudden insight, I pulled out my wand and let a little of my focus trickle down my arm into the comforting warm wood. The tip glowed clear white, distorting everyone's features, turning them into bogeymen, eyes lost in shadow. I angled the light down as Vicky murmured her delight at the show of magic, and I wondered what the hell she'd make of what was surely to come. I knew the vampires were here somewhere, but needed to play this cool for now.

My gut was right. The entrance was criss-crossed with the tire tracks of vehicles. One set looked like those of my current four by four, the others made by two vehicles, maybe three. They'd definitely planned this, had sent some vampires ahead on the long drive to arrive when needed, the rest coming through my damn front door. Then I remembered she'd had friends over earlier, the tracks could have been theirs, but usually they got dropped off, never entered the courtyard, so maybe I was right. I found it hard to think straight, but I knew the vampires were here. They had George.

"Okay, they're here," I said, "time to go stake some hearts."

"But I haven't got any stakes," moaned Vicky, looking panicked.

"I was joking, Vicky. You just have to kill them, that's all. I mean we. You stay here. The fun is over, this is life and death now, okay?"

"No." She stomped her foot, then spat out mud as it splattered all over her face and clothes.

"Please, I can't risk losing you. They're vampires. Actual, genuine, vampires. They'll kill you."

"I'm coming." My skinny friend stuck out her chest, shook her head so her ponytail bounced, and wiped at her face. She also remained right where she was.

"My dear lady, are you certain?" asked Nathan.
"Yes."

"Then take this, I have another." Nathan handed her a gun then jumped aside as she took it and waved it about.

"Hold that down," I hissed, grabbing her arm and lowering it.

"Sorry, I wasn't going to shoot you."

"Do you know how to use it?" asked Nathan, keeping well away from her.

"Um, not really."

"No matter. There's nothing to it. Just point it at bad guys and pull the trigger. So be careful, the safety's off."

"I can do that." Vicky nodded at me and repeated her words. "I can do that. I will."

"Fine. But stay behind us and if you need to use it wait until we aren't in your way. This is a last resort kind of thing." I worried she'd shoot herself in the foot, but that was better than her shooting me in the head.

I opened the gate and pushed it wide, and just as we were about to enter the farm proper a car pulled up. We tensed, but as it slowed Nathan said, "My people," and went to greet the new arrivals. Less than a minute later, we had three extra men, all clearly under Nathan's direct control. They were serious, and much larger than us, which was something.

"With no chance to formulate a proper plan, and time being of the essence, I suggest we approach this in a head-on, take no prisoners style of combat."

"Nathan, stop being a dick. Let's just go." I didn't wait. With magic thrumming through my system, my wand hot and almost squirming with anticipation of unleashing terrible forces, and my mind clouded with concern, I marched through my front gate, searching for monsters. And found them.

No Compromise

We spread out and slowly converged on the house. But the layout of the courtyard was such that there were plenty of hiding places where we could be ambushed before we got there. An old stable block was to the left, opposite the house, and there were storage barns at the far end that gave a clear line of sight to the gate.

Perfect setup for when I was in my house, not so perfect when the roles were reversed and I was the one approaching and unwelcome visitors had already arrived.

As if on cue, five vampires stepped out of the open stables one after the other like they were synchronized. More emerged from the old hay barn, and others came from the far end of the house, stepping forward into the light.

"Guess they're here then," I said to myself.

"Should I shoot them now?" asked Vicky, somehow having crept up beside me and taken what I had to admit was a pretty good shooting position.

"No. Save the bullets for when they're trying to rip out your throat."

"Oh, okay," she said chirpily, even though there was a tremor beneath it.

I gave her a curious look but she just said, "What?" and I honestly had no answer. Maybe she would make a good sidekick after all. She certainly wasn't afraid, or no more than anyone else.

"If you survive this then you're hired," I said, maybe talking just to hear my own voice. Needing the comfort, and her smile, to bolster my confidence and stop me utterly freaking out with worry about George. Everything felt too surreal, like it couldn't be happening. Anything but this, anything but George. We'd been safe for so long, nestled away and trying to muddle through, make a go of it as best we could. She was everything to me and I refused to accept she could come to harm. A world without her would be too empty to bear.

"Oh boy. Cool. So cool."

I turned, unbelieving. She wasn't, was she? She was!

"Vicky, please tell me you aren't doing your mom dance when we're about to fight vampires?"

"You know you think it's sexy."

Nathan gave me a puzzled look and spiraled a finger at his temple. I nodded in agreement. To my right, Brains studied Vicky like an interesting insect on a pin, then did something even stranger. He shuffled his shoulders and smiled. Then he moved closer, and with a nod to Vicky they did the terrible dance to the same silent beat, bumping hips.

"What? I like to dance," said Brains.

"You guys are nuts."

I stepped forward and out of the corner of my eye noted they stopped dancing and spread out again. As I moved, so did the vampires, all of them closing on us. Soon we were twenty feet or so apart, the atmosphere so tense you could taste the adrenaline in the air. I held up a hand and as I continued forward everyone behind me stopped. On the vampires' side all but one halted.

Forcing myself to walk, not run, to be calm not scream, I walked forward, my footsteps tapping on the ancient cobbles the only sound. The noise echoed off the buildings like the beating of a drum, signaling the end of my beautiful daughter's life and my grip on my waning sanity, until we were just a few feet apart. I was surprised Nathan had managed to stay out of it, but I guessed he wanted to see how they'd react and knew I was in no mood for his nonsense.

"This is private property," I said, my voice strong, no hint of the terror I felt inside.

"I know, and we apologize, but some things go beyond the usual rules. We are truly sorry."

He sounded like he meant it, but that didn't excuse the intrusion. The rules were clear for those in our world. You did not trespass. It was a declaration of war. But then, so was eating someone else's child, so I was taken aback by the apology.

"Do you have George, my daughter?"

The man shook, his whole body vibrating in that strange way they had where you could no longer tell what they were. It was as if they flowed through time differently, which I believe was the actual case. He suddenly stopped, looking truly mournful. "We do, but she will come to no harm. We regret this, Arthur, truly, but it's the only way to bring back Father, and we have no choice."

"There's always a choice. You've violated everything meant to be held dear by your kind. Your respect for others' privacy and the need for an invitation. The sanctity of home. You took my daughter and you expect mercy?"

He shook his head. "No, I do not. But this is our night, the beginning of a new era. I am Fourth, and soon I shall be Second. All of us shall be Seconds and our true power will spread across the globe and—"

I'd heard enough. I jabbed out fast with my wand, power surging through the wood with focused intent. The air alive with an angry, jagged sword of silver death that struck him in his chest and sent him flying across the courtyard into the arms of the others.

Still on his feet, he pushed against those that held him and looked down at the scorched flesh and the tattered clothes. Already he was repairing himself, just enough to stop the worst of the injury, but I knew it would be some time before he was properly mended. He was a Fourth, after all.

This would be easy. These guys weren't a match for me, for us. We'd be inside in less than a minute.

I advanced and those behind joined me.

We'd wipe the cobbles with them. Arm raised, magic radiating from my wand like a leaking tap, I readied to blast them to hell. Then I caught sight of the others with him, really looked at them.

Seconds, Thirds, and Fourths. Just because he was the spokesman, didn't mean he was in charge. He was the sacrifice if things went wrong.

It was gulp time. I did two.

Stained Cobbles

Never once in all the years I'd lived at the farm had blood been spilled on the cobbles. It was sacred. Mine, then mine and George's. Our sanctuary from this kind of horror.

But this night, with so much at risk, I was ready to stain it red with every last ounce of vampire blood I could squeeze from their bodies.

As the Fourth moved once more, he was stopped by the hand of another. An everyman, forgettable and plain. A Second. He didn't come forward, but he spoke.

"We truly do wish you no harm. Or your daughter. Please, allow us to complete the ritual and we shall leave. She is in no danger."

"So what's the plan? Sing some songs then release her?"

"I wish that were the case, but no. We must take her blood, but she will not be killed, or turned."

"They're lying, Arthur, we have to get the ashes now," said Nathan.

I turned to him and said, "Shut up. You don't care about her, you just want Mikalus. You're as bad as them. Worse."

"Please," shouted the Second, "we will be gone soon."

If that was the truth then it meant they were ready to use George to finish their ritual. "No, I can't, won't, let that happen. She's my daughter, my blood. Understand?"

"Yes," whispered the Second.

I believed him, felt and saw the truth he spoke, used the power I had within to look, really look. I saw him, I saw them all. Their auras weren't evil, just different. Colors never normally seen, so at odds were they with regular human beings. A purple light surrounded them, clean and pure in its own way, but so opposite to the norm it told a story of power, yet not evil or malice. Just of something different. With values altered by stretches of time hard to imagine for one as young as myself. Maybe if I lived to be their age I'd understand, but right now I didn't care.

"Last chance," I warned, part of me loath to kill, the other part, the part almost bubbling over, ready to go wild to get to George.

"Sorry," he said, and held his arms out to the side.

I turned to Vicky, Nathan, Brains, and the others and said, "We go to the door. If they stop us we kill them. Understand?" There were nods and the sounds of guns readied, and then we moved without another word.

With thirty feet of rough cobble between us and the door we walked as one, and then where once the space was clear it was now filled with vampires.

"They move really fast," said Vicky.

"Just shoot them," I replied with a sigh.

Wildcat magic, gunfire, shouts and screams filled the night, making a psychic stain on my home I could never scrub clean.

Reluctant Death

Encounters with vampires were usually brief, polite, and infrequent. Sure, there were issues. Fights, deaths, arguments, and certainly the Alliance had no love for them. But for all that, vampires were still of immense interest whether we liked to admit it or not. They were just so different, human yet not. They'd broken free of the constraints of the human body, had innate power, lived extended lives and could self-heal. The older they were, the better equipped they were to live through the ages and remain as they once were when human.

They adjusted, moved with the times. Lost their accents eventually if they lived in our country for too long, picked up British mannerisms and etiquette, and assimilated. They hid in plain sight, but, inevitably, such a life came with problems. They didn't age, not the old ones, so could never truly integrate.

But they had power, and they were mysterious, and we simply never knew the extent of their influence. We lived in our world, they in theirs.

Now wizard and vampire collided in a way that left me in no doubt about their nature.

They were strong as hell.

Nathan's spooks opened fire with automatic weapons that raked across the drab suits of the drab men, riddling them with bullets. The younger vampires dropped but were soon back up, the elders shook it off like the bullets were harmless gnats. Flesh repaired in moments, their bodies withstood the incredible pressure of a bullet hitting home and they walked forward right into the path of the assault.

As I tried to look everywhere at once, to keep track of them all, I knew it was useless and we were at a serious disadvantage. Even as I turned, I saw the first panic as a Fourth walked right up to him. The man froze for a moment then looked around wildly, but the vampire closed the remaining gap in less than a heartbeat and bit at his jugular. The vampire's cheeks bulged as the pressure exerted by the heart pumped out blood at an incredible rate, and then the vampire released its grip with a sick wet sound and the spook dropped, clutching feebly at his neck, pressure already easing as the last of his life force pumped erratically in a low arc, the first to stain the cobbles.

More deaths followed, the spooks taken out first by the least powerful vampires, still more than a match for humans with no power apart from guns.

Vicky fired off several rounds, hit a few vampires more by accident than skill, but soon realized it was fruitless and a waste of bullets she might need later. After that, she kept close and I focused on her and me.

It wasn't enough, though. The vampires acted as a unit, a pack, and the first thing a pack does is trap its prey, circle around back and cut off its means of escape. An attack from the rear is always more effective than a full-frontal assault, and that's exactly what they did. I forged ahead, Vicky to my left, her keeping it together enough to know not to get on my wand side. I dealt with the first few we encountered with a simple blast of energy that drained me a little but didn't take too much. All it did was slow them down, destroy flesh that quickly recovered.

I was holding back, not using enough to kill them outright as I didn't know what else I'd face. Once I'd drained myself utterly there would be no chance to regain my strength. It was the wrong move. My concern for George made me act out of character. From years of experience, I knew the best course of action in a fight was to go in hard, magic guns blazing, and wipe the floor with an opponent as fast and with as much deadly force as possible.

Cursing my own foolhardy actions, I changed tack and let the magic that was as much a part of me as my beating heart consume me utterly. There was no point showing restraint in case I needed my strength later—if I didn't pull out all the stops now there would be no later. There would be only death. Maybe I'd get another life, maybe I wouldn't. But with my daughter's life in danger now wasn't the time to risk it.

I surrendered to the power I'd spent a lifetime absorbing, that had permeated the very essence of my being. Nothing left in reserve, a total immersion in the abilities I'd mastered best I could. This level of violence was not something I needed to call on much. The work I did was dangerous, but there are always degrees of danger, and usually a quick blast with the wand did the trick.

Not this time, not now. Not with so much to lose.

It's Magic, Baby

Regular sight was replaced with an awareness beyond explanation. If you've never experienced it then you cannot even imagine it. It's like having a multitude of eyes pointing in every direction, all feeding back information at incredible speed. Providing an image of everything around you. Every fine detail, every gesture, every anticipated movement, so detailed and rich, so beyond what we normally see, it's almost like the world becomes thought.

What was Arthur expanded to become something else. Cognizance, with knowledge of actions yet performed, read through slight adjustments in body position, facial tics and a glance this way or that you don't even know you're doing.

I could anticipate each and every movement of every character at play in this deadly drama and I used that knowledge to unleash dangerous forces in one plane of existence whilst being half in another. Time to go inside my own goddamn house.

Magic comes in endless forms, shaped by your intent and your will, your skill and your personality. Often, I was a blast 'em type of guy. It's quick, effective, and freaks people out. But I knew spells, could conjure up a beastie if I felt the need, and could harness strange, unexplained forces that permeated the universe if I really focused and the juices were flowing.

The juices were definitely flowing.

With great focus and determination it's incredible what the human mind and spirit is capable of. Add to that one wildcat wizard with his entire being soaked in magic and laser-like intent and you get one helluva dangerous combination.

My mind emptied of everything but my goal, to destroy those in my path. I called out to the air, the gaps between it, and as I focused the power inside through my body and directed it into base reality via the glowing wand, I willed those gaps to expand.

With a wild roar, I pushed out as hard as I could at the space between me and the vampires spread out in a circle and prised apart the gaps. The air rippled, the light dancing widely, increasing patches of darkness expanding as where there was no matter there was no light, no gravity, nothing.

No air, no sound, no anything.

An emptiness that I forced my will into. A pocket of nothingness that was silent and still. I spun hard and fast, trailing my wand behind me, once, twice, three times. Pushing out from our small group at the vampires, the tiny pinpricks of nothingness, the base nature of everything, there before there was any form of matter, when there was no universe, no thought, no creation, expanded and chewed through their bodies.

No, not chewing, merely replacing. Where once was a solid creature, there were now gaps. I shunted all I could out through the wand to push harder at the emptiness, and it grew, taking out more and more pieces of the vampires. At first it was little but black dots, hardly giving them pause. They closed in, wary now as the magic thrummed and the air crackled then fell silent, then tiny pops burst in the air from all directions, sound pockets exploding then eaten away like the light, like their bodies.

"Get close to me," I shouted as the air screamed with the dangerous disruptions. Within our small circle it eddied and pulled at us, all of us touching now, only my arm extended out from the tight mass of flesh.

The vampires shouted, then screamed, then tried to get to us, but I held my focus, kept on pushing, and the darkness, the void, expanded, splashes of emptiness dotting their bodies. Tiny gaps appeared in their flesh where you could see right through.

The younger ones collapsed, trying to regenerate, repair what was missing, but as fast as they did so I let the non-matter chew away more of them until eventually it hit heart or brain and it was over.

Only three remained and they were the most powerful. A Second and two Thirds—I knew this to be the case although I couldn't explain how. They retreated, my power weaker the further away they moved, and I took the opportunity to shuffle slowly to the front door. I reached out for the wards expecting them to be broken, only to find most still intact. But there were gaps in the protection, areas of carnage. Someone with real strength had pushed the wards aside enough to allow the vampires entry. My house was meant to be impenetrable.

"Wait for my signal then get inside as fast as possible," I said through clenched teeth. Nathan nodded, Brains likewise, and Vicky replied, "Whenever you say."

I readied to take down the wards but at that precise moment the three vampires attacked. I pushed out against them, gave everything to force apart the reality of this world and destroy them, but the pockets of the void I created were smaller than before, my hold weakening, and they were so fast, connected to the vibrations I emitted, that they weaved between the gaps, impossibly fast, and were on us.

Running on Empty

"Wait," I shouted, but Vicky was closest to the door and must have thought I'd given a signal when I nodded. I hadn't, I'd just changed focus to negate the wards. In a panic of trying to stop the vampires sucking us dry. My magic faltering, and Vicky almost at the door, I pulled back the wards with steely focus, picturing the protection as floating, burnt umber sigils peeling away and gliding to hover over my head.

But it was too late, and moments before they were completely removed she shoved at the door. It opened and she toppled inside, screaming and crying as she crashed down onto the old rug and banged her head hard, the thin material nowhere near enough of a cushion to stop her getting an almighty crack to the temple.

Distracted, I felt the presence of a Second, breath on my neck, and jabbed an elbow into his kidney, buying myself a moment. Brains was still in human form, probably knowing his wild side couldn't deal with the magic chewing away at reality, and Nathan, well, he'd decided to use his cane. He cracked down hard on a Third's head then I saw it glow white-hot as magic spat out a spasm of intense heat that made the vampire's head burst into flames.

As the others were distracted, I ushered Nathan and Brains through the door and I slammed down the wards while the vampires started to recover.

Too late, they were inside with us, everyone falling over themselves as they shoved but nobody had room to move.

The Third, scalp blasted, hair in patches but already regenerating, shoved Brains and he toppled forward, knocking against Nathan. They both stumbled, off-balance. I backed up, only to see the door closing.

This was it, now or never. With what strength remained I muttered to myself, giving my aching limbs a good talking to, and raised my wand, readying all I had left, to kill those that would stop me getting George.

One final push, just enough to kill them, and we'd be clear. My arm raised, the vampires pushed forward, a sadness in their eyes, not wanting to cause our deaths but willing to nonetheless. Magic spasmed down my arm, connecting me to the wand through a bond forged over years.

"Enough," came a voice of authority from the far end of the hall where it opened out into the kitchen.

I turned, and let the magic fade. Through the opening I saw nine vampires standing in a circle, one space empty. George was standing at the center, looking scared and alone like a small child. A Second stood beside her, held her firmly yet without violence. The Second I'd given the ashes to.

There they were, beside them in the center. A simple wooden box containing the cause of this nightmare I'd been dragged into.

"No more violence," said the Second, almost whispering, his voice carrying easily through the silence. "We will not harm her, Arthur, but if you do not cease this madness you will be killed, and your daughter will no longer have a father. Do you understand me?"

"You can't trust them," said Nathan, eyes darting from me to the box, his reason lost, so consumed with lust for the power it contained was he.

"Shut up, Nathan," I said.

"Yeah, shut up, Nathan," said Brains, lowering his arms, nodding to me.

Nathan may have been willing to risk leaving George fatherless, at the mercy of the vampires, but I wasn't. Following Brains' lead, I lowered my arm, and pocketed my wand.

"Come, you may be present at the rebirth of Father," said the Second, beckoning us forward with a cold smile. There was a hardness in his eyes that told us he would destroy everyone if we interfered again.

With no choice, knowing now wasn't the time to risk everything, I wandered down my hallway, noting as if for the first time that it was in need of a good tidy. Books were in piles against the bookcase, those on it in disarray, and the few important items that sat on the shelves were covered with dust. Strange what you focus on in times of stress. I'd have to shout at the maid, i.e. me.

I just had to bide my time, wait for an opportunity. Or maybe, just maybe, they were telling the truth and they wouldn't kill George and the rest of us.

It didn't matter. If they thought I'd let them feed from my daughter then they didn't know The Hat at all.

It Comes to This

"Are you okay?" I asked George as we walked into the kitchen, the mingled scents of coffee and pine kitchen cleaner so familiar yet so incongruous when tainted by the stench of vampires. I could smell their excitement, taste it on the gentle breeze that came through the open doors. The air danced with otherworldly energy, building as they focused on their goal, now so close they were almost in a trance. So intent were they on the small box, our presence was little but a minor distraction. Like a fly buzzing about in another room when you want to concentrate.

"Been better," said George, giving me a smile despite her obvious terror.

"Lightweight," I replied, winking. I turned at a noise, only to see the vampires pick up Vicky carefully and take her into the den.

They emerged a moment later and one said, "She'll be fine. Just stunned by the wards and the bump to the head."

I nodded, then turned back to the circle and the Second still holding George. Her upper arm was white where he gripped tight, and that hint of possible harm set my blood to boiling. How dare he touch her? How dare they desecrate the sanctity of my home?

"You can fight," said the Second, reading my thoughts easily, "or you can watch. Be assured your daughter is safe, and then it will be over and we will leave."

"Look at you, dressed in your finest blood robes, all pompous and full of self-importance. But you're nothing but animals. Scaring young girls, breaking all the rules your kind and mine have abided by for so long. You disgrace yourselves and deserve to die." Without realizing, I was walking forward, but the vampires that survived the fight placed themselves in my way. I glared at them, daring them to try anything. The truce was broken, I couldn't let this happen.

"Arthur, please. This is too important. Don't you understand? This is who we are. Mikalus is the Father, our maker. We have the chance after so many years, so many endless, lonely centuries to bring him back. See him again, feel his love. We cannot be denied this. We will not be denied this. Do you understand me?"

"I understand. But know this, you have made an enemy. I will not forgive you."

"As you wish." He nodded and my way was clear. I moved forward, Nathan and Brains joining me. "Remain outside the circle and do not interfere. You may stay to ensure we keep our word. But if you set foot inside, it will not go well for you, for your friends, or for her." The Second revealed his teeth, a warning, and I got the message loud and clear.

I was impotent with rage, with concern for George, but understood I'd lose.

Yet I knew there was no option; I had to go down fighting. Whatever they promised, I knew they would ruin her, would turn her or kill her. Once they began their resurrection they would be consumed with bloodlust, lose themselves to their feeding, and George's life would be over.

I would not stand by and let that happen.

As I focused what little magic still vibrated in my system, prepared to at least try, all I could think was that my life hadn't been so bad, that I had only one regret. That I hadn't been able to protect my daughter. I'd failed her when she needed me most.

"I love you, George. But I wish you'd answer your damn phone when I call."

"Love you, Dad." She knew this was it, but she didn't cry, didn't fall to pieces. She straightened her back, smiled weakly, and I was more proud of her then than I'd ever been.

I felt the tension of the vampires build. They knew what I was about to do, and would tear me to shreds. So be it. The Hat did not negotiate with kidnappers, The Hat went wild on the abusers of children.

I felt a hand on my shoulder. Time was up.

A Sacrifice

"Take me," said Brains, nodding at me as I turned, then stepping forward into the circle. "Take me in her place."

"That's very kind of you," said the Second, "but this must be done as laid down in the book."

"I know the book. I know all about Mikalus, and I know all about you." Brains sounded different, he was talking in more than one word sentences for a start.

"What do you know?" asked the Second, raising an eyebrow.

"I know you've got it wrong, that you'll fail if you use this child." Brains stood tall, oozing confidence. He was sure of what he said, and it made the vampires, all of them, pause.

The Second nodded to his aides and they took hold of George, not cruelly, not harshly, not hurting her, but they held her nonetheless. He walked like the invisible man over to Brains and I thought he was going to walk right on through him, only stopping inches from his face. The Second looked Brains up and down, inspecting him, going past the outward appearance and delving deeper. Looking inside the man at what he truly was.

"You have been hurt terribly. You are broken, damaged. I'm sorry, humans can be so cruel, none are crueler. I can take away that pain, you can join us, become one of us, but we must resurrect the First and you cannot help with that. Man-wolf, you must know that much as it hurts you here," the Second thumped his heart, "sometimes sacrifices must be made."

"Look closer," said Brains. "Look at me, truly look, and tell me what you see?"

"I see a man abused by another, for many long years. I see a man who should be broken yet stands tall. I see a man who has lost everything yet his will is strong, his soul pure..." The Second trailed off, words faltering.

"Unsullied, and touched by the universe. Right?"

Damn, what was happening? Brains had been used and abused by Merrick for years as far as I could gather, was a lycanthrope and the right-hand man of a gangster. He was far from unsullied, far from pure, certainly not touched by the universe.

"You are a strange one," admitted the Second. "True, you have a pure soul, for what you have done was for love. You have not been taken by that man, not in a carnal way, not like that, and you are touched by the universe, for you are unique. You are more than just a man, have the magic of the universe inside you."

"See, I told you. You cannot use the girl. She's an innocent and hasn't agreed to this. I agree. I will be the one to help you get what you want."

"No, it saddens me no end, but it must be her."

"All my life I've searched for answers to what I am, to uncover the truth about the world. I know magic. I know the good guys, like Arthur, and the bad, like my dead boss, and have seen the worst mankind can do to one another. You're not like that, not human, are more. But you're not cruel, just different like me. Am I right?"

The Second thought for a moment and answered carefully. "We are all different. Some of us are good, others bad, such is life. But the Children of the Blood are not inherently wicked, we are merely vampire. We are unique, yes. Inhuman but not inhumane. We don't crave dominion over others, wish only to have Father return. To have him lead us, show us the path, allow us to all be Seconds. Become his children once more and be as close to him as possible."

"I understand," said Brains. "So take me. I know the prophecy, and it will not work if you take the girl against her will. I'm touched by the universe, am pure of heart if not actions, and unsullied for the cruelties inflicted on me have never touched my core. You can see this, you know."

The Second nodded and the nine others murmured their agreement.

I thought I was dreaming, that something had gone screwy in my head and this was just wishful thinking. Maybe I was dead, playing out the scenario as

I bled out on my kitchen floor. But no, this was real, this was happening.

George was released and she ran to me. I wrapped her in my arms and she clung to me like I wished I could have experienced when she was a child. Oh, how I wished I had been there, to hug her and lift her up and buy her ice cream. But I had her now, and that was what counted.

"Dad, you came. I thought you'd be too late."

"If you'd answered your phone this could have been avoided," I said, smiling at her.

"Forgot to charge it." George moved back and said, "Can't you please let him go?"

"It's all right. Trust me, I've had worse things happen," said Brains.

"Haven't we all?" I said, nodding at him.

"Let us begin," said the Second.

It Begins

I couldn't even begin to think of the sacrifice Brains was making. I'd got him totally wrong, and again wondered what the hell Merrick had done to have such a hold over him. Whatever it was, it didn't look like I'd ever get the answer as he was about to get sucked on by ten vampires.

And they themselves were a revelation. They weren't barbarous, not really. They were believers in a religion. More. It surpassed that, for they had proof, real proof that what they believed in was real. They were proof of the existence of the First, and there he was, in a simple, small wooden box on the floor in my kitchen, the moon shining through the open doors, the space lit up by overhead recessed lights.

The vampires held no malice, weren't evil or vindictive, just different. All this runaround, the death, the chasing and the intrusion was unwelcome to say the least. They had threatened my daughter, were willing to do what it took to get what they wanted, but they weren't going to kill her, just needed her.

Brains had offered himself up as he knew she'd never be the same again if they each bit her. That she would be tortured for the rest of her life by such an act. Would be scared, have nightmares, unable to be a young girl and maybe have a bright future as it would leave too much of a stain on a still impressionable mind.

He was willing to sacrifice himself. He was performing an act of kindness. He already had his scars, he wanted to ensure George never got any.

Holding George's hand, never wanting to let go, I glanced over at Nathan as the preparations were made. He was beaten, you could see it in his face. He was resigned to what was about to happen, and he was livid.

I saw him tap away on his phone for a moment then sigh and nod absently as he got a reply. We wandered over, seemingly forgotten by the vampires now they were so close to their end goal.

"There gonna be trouble?" I asked, nodding at the phone held tight in his hand.

"No, no trouble. I called them off, sent everyone back. It's just us."

"What, not gonna try to kill them all, get the ashes and lock them away for yourselves somewhere dark and suitably secure where you can go look and revel in how brilliant you guys are?"

"You've made your point, no need to rub it in. No, it's over because short of blowing the place up there's no way we can stop this now."

"There's always the open doors," I said, nodding at the far end of the kitchen.

"An open door doesn't mean you can just come in uninvited, am I right?"

"Haha, yeah, the wards will still fry your ass."

"Exactly. No, this time, Arthur, I'm afraid I didn't get my own way. This whole sorry mess has been very taxing, it's time to go."

"Not hanging around for the grand finale?" I asked.

"Arthur, you really have no clue, do you?" he asked, giving me a peculiar look.

"Enlighten me."

"I am a Second in my own right, of Cerberus. I have seen more, done more, than you could possibly imagine. Over the years, I have witnessed such wondrous things, can walk into a room and touch the wonders of heaven and earth. I know the secrets of the government, am involved in every aspect of how this country and many others run. I'm not interested in this, not enough anyway. Who knows what will happen if they succeed?"

"Haha, not interested enough to risk getting killed, you mean? Not enough to stick around and see what happens just in case you get the life sucked out of you for interfering?"

"Yes, there is that. Goodbye, Arthur, I'll be in touch."

"Oh, goodie, can't wait."

"My dear." Nathan nodded at George and then he skirted the circle of chanting vampires and turned when he reached the threshold. I nodded, let down the wards for a moment, still not trusting him to not have a bunch of spooks ready to pounce, and once he stepped over I slammed them back into place.

It was just us now. Me, George, a load of vampires, Brains, and a box of ash on the kitchen floor.

They began to feed.

A Gentleness

Brains was stripped to the waist and standing beside the ashes. The vampires were all dressed in simple red robes—hey, everyone likes to dress for special occasions, right?

One stepped forward and with a world of sadness behind her eyes she caressed the ravaged body of Brains. He shuddered, the delicate touch of the woman's slender fingers over his flesh sensual, that of a careful lover. She traced the scars across his chest and stood on tiptoe to whisper words meant just for him.

He nodded, and smiled down at her.

She bent and put her mouth to a healthy part of his flesh and the others gasped. Brains winced and cried out quietly as his skin was broken. The woman held her position for a few moments then released and stood. She moaned, "Thank you," just loud enough for us to hear, and as she retreated I saw the blood at her mouth, smeared ruby red. Gentle trickles stained Brain's pale flesh then fell like tears from two delicate puncture wounds.

George gripped me tight, squeezing hard, but she didn't look away and I didn't try to make her. Some things are best seen, rather than imagined, and this was one.

The next stepped forward, a man, the Second I knew, and he too whispered and Brains nodded before the ritual was performed again.

Eight times more it happened, each one gentle and considerate, no violence of any sort. No malice or cruelty, the vampires caressing his flesh and telling him he was no damaged man, that they loved him and adored him. He was the key to their own future and for that they would always be in his debt.

The circle was completed once more and the vampires held hands, Brains still at the center. They had not turned him, had taken not given him their venom. They had not violated him in any way he hadn't offered.

"You may join us," said the woman who fed first.

"We will always love you. You will be with family. We will be you. You will be us."

Brains nodded. Then he smiled.

I wanted to cry out, and George gasped beside me, but I told her quietly, "All anyone wants is a family. To belong. He's finally found his."

The woman moved to him and took his hand, lifted his arm to her mouth. Her teeth dripped the clear venom of the vampire, known as the Immortal Tear. She held his gaze as she bit his wrist and gave something of herself to him.

"Be the first," she said, and she joined the others, holding hands once again as they completed the circle.

Brains nodded, and with his wrist dripping blood all over my clean tiles he took three steps to the box, bent, and slid the lid aside. He lifted his arm and I watched, entranced, as several drops of blood now of the vampire landed softly in the ashes.

The vampires gasped and they broke the circle as Brains took the place of one that stepped forward, taking the hands either side of him to complete the circle.

They repeated it until finally there was just one more left to give blood.

He held his hand over the box, bit his wrist, and the blood poured down his fingers, hanging tantalizingly for the longest time. The bead became fat and swollen on his middle finger, and then a single drop fell and landed in the ashes to mingle with that of the others.

He glanced in, smiled, and moved fast back to the others where he resumed his position. Watching from behind the vampires, I saw smoke rise from the box, and then it hissed. The wood fell away revealing a pile of wet, gray mush, steaming and bubbling.

It expanded, the mess darkening until it was black. And then it spread out, growing as it did so.

Slowly, the color changed, and it moved again, rolling up into endless thin strands that looked like hair.

It was hair! It grew long until it looked like a wig on my floor—which was weird, I can tell you—then the hair rose and a forehead appeared. Soon, the closed eyes of a man could be seen, then a nose, then a full head. It kept on growing, revealing a skeletal torso, bones covered in flesh that filled out a little as the man rose from the ashes.

Finally, it was a complete man. Naked, well over six feet tall, painfully thin, hair as dark as night falling down to his waist. Mikalus was old and frail and yet he changed even as we watched. The years shrank from him, until he was a scrawny forty-something, weak as a kitten, muscles wasted away but a semblance of youth restored.

As nails grew on his toes and the resurrection completed, his mouth opened wide and he screamed, letting out the hurt of a thousand years of suffering, of a death that gave no peace. It told of unimaginable, endless torment, and of his happiness, his confusion, his lack of understanding, but mostly of the unbridled joy of being reborn, having a voice to air his raw emotions.

After what felt like a lifetime, the screaming stopped. Mikalus opened his eyes, the gunk around them stretching then breaking, revealing eyes so blue and intense they almost shone.

Mikalus smiled.

"My children," he croaked with utter adoration only a parent could understand. A thousand years he had been in torment, away from his children. Now they were reunited.

He toppled to the floor, unable to hold himself upright on his emaciated muscles.

"Guess they didn't have a gym in hell," I whispered to George.

"Dad!" She punched me on the arm.

We'd be all right.

Goodbye to New Friends

The spell was broken and the vampires, Brains included, ran to Mikalus. Then time lost meaning as everything happened so fast. They dressed Mikalus in regular clothes and all got dressed themselves.

Phones were used, spreading the news worldwide within the vampire community, and the kitchen was alive with noise like an impromptu party had sprung up. It was bewildering and confusing and somehow beautiful to have watched, been a non-participating part of.

The Second I knew came over to us and said, "Thank you, thank you so much. I apologize for my actions, for all of our behavior. Sometimes it's hard to be a good person when you want something so badly. You lose yourself, lose your dignity and your sense of what is right and wrong."

"Happens to the best of us," I said, knowing that was the damn truth.

"And to you, dear George, I apologize most of all. It wasn't our intent to harm you, but I know you were scared. I'm sorry."

He didn't wait for a reply, didn't expect to be absolved. Knew what he'd done and merely wanted to apologize.

"You okay?" I asked, putting my arm around her and squeezing.

"Been better. You?"

"Yeah, had better days. While the apologies are going around, I want to say sorry, too. Can you forgive me? For bringing all this here, to our home? I want you to be safe, more than anything. I thought being here would keep you away from this kind of thing. I was wrong, I'm sorry."

"It's okay, Dad. Don't sweat it."

"Oh, and one more thing. Who's the boy? I saw how nervous you were when they talked about being unsullied. You might be able to fool a vampire but you can't fool me."

"Dad!"

"What? Just tell me his name so I can go kill him."

"You would, wouldn't you?"

"Try me. You're my daughter."

"You're such a sneak. Thought you'd trick me, didn't you? Don't worry, I'm still waiting to find the right guy."

"Good. Wait until I'm dead and gone and I'll die a happy man. Boys are trouble, all of them. Trust me, I was one."

"Still are," she said, smiling.

I caught sight of Brains and said, "Give me a moment?" George nodded and I moved over to him. Most of the vampires were ready to leave, coming and going easily now I'd dropped the wards. Seemed rather pointless given the circumstances.

I nodded at a few as they smiled thanks before leaving, the numbers dwindling fast. Mikalus was nowhere to be seen, presumably already whisked away somewhere safe. Guess maybe they'd use my front door back to the city, or maybe not. I definitely had to have words with Sasha about her supposedly updated wards. What use were they if they didn't stop unwanted guests? And more to the point, where the hell was she? It's at exactly times likes this a guy needed his faery godmother around. That's the fae for you, flaky as hell.

"Brains," I said as he stopped in front of me.

"Arthur. Thank you."

"I should be the one thanking you, for stepping in for George. That was a brave thing you did there, and I gotta say, surprising. How did you know it would work?"

Brains leaned in close, then checked nobody was near enough to hear. "It's superstition, Arthur. Sure, I believed they could resurrect Mikalus. I do know a lot about the vampires, and about many magical or supernatural things, but these prophecies, these rituals, they were written by someone long after Mikalus died. Words get corrupted, lost in translation. Are open to interpretation."

"You mean you bluffed?" I couldn't believe it. He'd risked so much and he wasn't even sure it would work. "What if you'd been wrong?"

"George would have still had a chance. I didn't doubt you'd have done something to save her. Or tried. Yes, I bluffed. Kind of. Merrick never did... you know. But he did other things. Worse things. I'm no saint, but he took me when I was young, before I had the chance to find love, even affection, so I guess that in the antiquated language of the prophesy I am unsullied. Anyway, I, er... I winged it. All they needed was fresh blood of a human mixed with their own. His children, ten of them and one human's, that's all. Anyone could have taken my place."

"You are one ballsy dude, Brains."

"Ivan, my name's Ivan."

I nodded. "Ivan it is. And a vampire."

"Yes, and a vampire. That's what I'm thanking you for. For allowing me to find a family at last. To belong."

"Everyone belongs somewhere, Ivan. I'm glad you found your family."

"Me too," he said, watching with me as most of the Seconds left, nodding to us as they did so.

"What now? I asked, wishing I knew more about this man and what had happened, but smart enough to know this wasn't the time.

"Now? Now I go with them for a few hours. Then I kill most of Merrick's men. The cruel ones, the bad men. Then I'll return to the vampires to be led through my transformation and when I am truly vampire, after the blood is changed, I'll accept the fresh blood of Mikalus, making me a Second."

"So no more gangster stuff?"

"Haha. Oh, Arthur, what else is there? This is the only world I know, and I have to admit," he said slyly, "I relish the excitement. No, I'll clean house then run things differently. Change things. It won't be perfect, and there are hard decisions to be made, but I'm a fair man. There will be no more acts of foulness under my watch."

"A man with a plan." What could I say? Guess anything would be better than Merrick.

"I've waited a long time for this, for my freedom. Who knew it would happen like this? And it seems that being in charge will be good for both me and the vampires. A new dawn is coming, Arthur. We are both here to witness it." Ivan winked at me and waved goodbye as he departed with the last of the vampires.

It may have been a new dawn, but I had concerns about being there at dusk. Ah well, all you can do is enjoy the day and let the rest take care of itself.

I brought up the wards, not that there seemed much point, but old habits die hard, and George and I walked to the back door and listened until the last vehicles departed.

We stood there for a while watching the moon, my arm around her shoulder, hers around my waist, and then I slid the doors closed.

Halfway back across the kitchen I remembered something. I stopped and said, "I've got a gift for you."

"A gift?"

I unfastened the pocket in my cargo pants and pulled out the neatly wrapped package I'd been given in exchange for the ashes of Mikalus.

"For you," I said, as I handed it to a confused looking George.

A Gift

There are some things money cannot buy, and true love is one of them. Family is another. Also rare wands that are beyond priceless. This was what Nigel had offered me for the ashes, and I should have said no. Such things were immensely valuable, beyond my means and rarely for sale for money, but for favors. I couldn't refuse when I told him I'd do the mystery job if he got me what I wanted in return.

Was the trade worth it? Who knew? Only time would tell. I'd handed over the most infamous vampire in history, but the look on George's face was priceless.

"A wand? Oh, er thanks."

"Not just any wand," I declared grandly. "It's Tinkerbell's wand."

"Haha, shut up." I waited for her to stop smiling and she stared at me for the longest time. "You're serious? Really? You did this for me? You got it for me?"

"Of course. I'd do anything for you."

"You remembered?"

"I remember everything when it comes to you, George. I love you."

When George was young, a few years old I guess, I'd bumped into her mother on the street. She was already pretty far gone, hanging out with a group of other women. There were lots of kids, all underfed, all craving love and attention. It had broken my heart, knowing the children had little hope of a good future, and I didn't stay long.

I had no idea one of the children was even hers, let alone mine, and she never said, obviously. But for a few minutes I spent time with this grubby little kid prancing about with a stick saying she was Tinkerbell and she was gonna be a real faery when she grew up. I smiled and basically ignored the manic creature that may as well have been from another planet. I wasn't a fan and had zero experience of children, not that I had much more now, and that was that.

But I remembered. When George turned up and told me who she was I recalled that day and knew it was the same girl. That first night, we spent hours sitting in the dark in the den, talking non-stop until dawn broke over the farm. Then she joined me to take care of the animals.

As we let out the chickens for the day, I asked her if she still liked Tinkerbell and she blushed scarlet, asking me nervously how I knew. I told her the story and she said, yeah, it was silly, and girly, but she still read the books and it was still her goal in life to have a powerful wand just like Tinkerbell. She was already dabbling in magic by then, guess it ran in the blood.

She swore me to secrecy, said I was never to tell another soul, and that she felt foolish. I told her never to feel foolish for dreaming, for believing, and anything she wanted in life she would get if she worked for it hard enough.

George lifted the slender wand, inspected it closely, and said, "Thank you, Dad."

"My pleasure. It was a breeze. Anything for my girl. My daughter. Come on, Vicky's lying out cold in the living room, let's go wake her up."

"She's gonna be so annoyed she missed all the action," chuckled George.

"Hey, no rubbing it in," I warned. "I'm never gonna hear the last of this and I think I may have told her she could be my new sidekick."

"Haha, rather you than me. Thanks, Dad." George hugged me tight and that made everything all right in the world.

Kids, eh? Wish she'd said she wanted a bike.

The End

19926951R00188

Printed in Great Britain
by Amazon